SUBMITTING TO DOM

CW00515378

The Martinis and Chocolate Book Club 4

Lara Valentine

EVERLASTING CLASSIC

Siren Publishing, Inc.
www.SirenPublishing.com

A SIREN PUBLISHING BOOK
IMPRINT: Everlasting Classic

SUBMITTING TO THE DEVIL DOM
Copyright © 2013 by Lara Valentine

ISBN: 978-1-62740-343-6

First Printing: July 2013

Cover design by Les Byerley
All art and logo copyright © 2013 by Siren Publishing, Inc.

ALL RIGHTS RESERVED: This literary work may not be reproduced or transmitted in any form or by any means, including electronic or photographic reproduction, in whole or in part, without express written permission.

All characters and events in this book are fictitious. Any resemblance to actual persons living or dead is strictly coincidental.

Printed in the U.S.A.

PUBLISHER
Siren Publishing, Inc.
www.SirenPublishing.com

SUBMITTING TO THE DEVIL DOM

The Martinis and Chocolate Book Club 4

LARA VALENTINE
Copyright © 2013

Chapter One

His hand trailed down her belly and between her legs, pausing to swirl around her clit before pressing a finger deep inside her. Lori cried out from the intense sensation, and he smiled, knowing she loved the feeling of being filled. For weeks he had refused to fuck her, preserving her virgin status, if only technically. He wanted her to be desperate for him.

"Please. Please, Cal. I need you to fuck me."

He shook his head, licking her abdomen. "No. Not until we're married."

"We don't even have a date yet," she sobbed in protest. "Don't you want me?"

He wrapped his hand around her neck and pulled her face close to his. "If I wanted you any more, woman, I'd fucking explode into a million pieces. I'm going to bring you to release over and over tonight. You won't have any doubt in your mind I find you the most beautiful, sexy woman in the world."

She pressed her lips to his, her mouth tasting of coffee and apples. She ran her fingers down his back and pressed herself close. "Please, Cal. I can't wait."

Cal smiled, running a finger across her lips to distract her. He reached behind him and flicked a switch on the table that was connected to a small camera hidden among his cluttered bookshelves. His little Lori had no idea it was there. It was more exciting this way.

"Are you sure, love? Are you sure you want to do this? I need you to convince me."

She tugged at the buttons on his shirt. "Then I'll say it straight out. I want you to fuck me. Fuck me hard, Cal. Make me your woman."

Cal pressed her back on the bed, sparing only a glance in the camera's direction. "I will, baby. Tonight is one that will never be forgotten."

Tori Cordell tucked her dark brown hair behind her ear and tossed her e-reader on the table with a sigh of disgust. "What an asshole. What a complete and total douche bag."

Lisa Hart sipped her Cosmo. She was a beautiful, tanned blonde who adored her husband and children and took out her aggressions on defenseless lumps of clay turning them into works of art. "He's definitely not hero material, that's for sure. I'm not sure how this author is going to redeem him in the end. So far, he's been nothing but a jerk."

Sara Jameson, quiet, dark haired and petite, checked on her son, Jonah, in the portable play yard. He was nine months old now and crawling everywhere when he was awake. Blessedly, he was sleeping peacefully at the moment, looking completely angelic. "Maybe we'll get to see him really grovel. I love it when a man grovels."

"Do Jeremy and Cole know about this?" Brianne teased. Brianne Hart had auburn hair and sparkling green eyes that could turn a stormy gray if she was angry. She had the mama-bear personality of the group and would come to the defense of her friends and loved ones without question. "They don't look like the groveling type to me."

Sara rolled her eyes. "They're not. Luckily, they rarely have anything to grovel about. My husbands are almost perfect."

"Hey," Noelle Hunter protested. Noelle's personality was as fiery as her red hair. She was fun and impetuous, and she kept their book-club meetings interesting. "My husband is pretty perfect, too."

Tori laughed and raised her glass to the webcam. Noelle was attending the book club over Skype, as she now lived in Montana with her brand-new husband, Cam Hunter. "Your husband is pretty darn close to perfect. But, well, my new boyfriend is really something, as well."

She had everyone's attention. Lisa practically jumped out of her chair. "You've been keeping secrets, young lady. You better start talking. We had no idea you were seeing someone. How long has this been going on?"

Tori sipped her pomegranate martini with a smile. She'd been waiting for the perfect moment to spring this on her friends. It was a big deal. She hadn't had a date, a real date, for over a year. Until now.

"Remember I told you about my new neighbor, Ian Taggert? The police detective? Well, we started spending quite a bit of time together. Dinner at each other's house, swimming, even trips to the mall and grocery store. He finally asked me out on what he called a 'real damn date,' and it was wonderful." Tori smiled as she remembered the hot kiss they had shared at the end of the evening. Ian was totally gorgeous and a great kisser, to boot. "Long story short, we've been formally dating each other for about three weeks. He's smart, funny, and sexy. I feel like I've won the lottery."

Noelle laughed and popped a chocolate into her mouth. "I knew you were next. When do we get to meet this paragon of virtue?"

"If you play your cards right, today. I signed for a package for him today, and he sent a text earlier saying he might stop by after work and pick it up."

Brianne waggled her eyebrows. "We want the dirty details. Have you slept with him yet? Was it hot?"

Despite being the mother of two grown sons, Tori blushed. She'd never had a hot sex life to discuss with her friends before. "No, not yet. We've kissed and done some, oh, I guess you would call it heavy petting. He knows that I've been celibate since Carl died. Let's face it. I've dated some real losers in the past few years."

Major understatement. The men she'd dated either wanted a mother, a maid, or a one-night stand. She wasn't interested in being any of those things with a man. She wanted a man who could be an equal partner. Mostly, she wanted to have some fun. She'd been a wife and mother by the time she was eighteen. At thirty-six, she was ready to start living her own life and enjoying it.

She wanted a man who could have fun in life and be an adventurer in the bedroom. Carl had been a good husband but a tad staid in the lovemaking department. He'd been the epitome of the gentle lover even when she'd wanted to be ravished. Ian looked the ravish type, if there was such a thing.

The ring of the doorbell interrupted her thoughts and brought a smile to her face. It was just about the right time for Ian to be stopping by. She'd missed him all day. Their goodnight kiss last night had been achingly hot and had made her want to beg him to sweep her off her feet and into his bedroom.

"Tori, sweetheart, are you in here?" Ian came striding into the living room with a sexy smile. As usual, her heart sped up, and her stomach, along with something a little lower, started to flutter. He was absolutely gorgeous.

At an inch over six feet tall, he was the perfect height. His body was honed to muscular perfection by his regular, intense workouts. He looked devastatingly handsome with blond hair clipped short, a square jaw with a dimpled chin, and sparkling blue eyes. She drank in the sight of him like a thirsty woman in the desert. She could stare at him all day long and not get bored.

"I'm here, Ian. My book club is here, too. I want you to meet them."

She stood and headed straight for him. She wasn't a big fan of public displays of affection, but she couldn't imagine not greeting him with a kiss. He leaned forward and gave her a peck on the cheek, obviously not comfortable going for it in front of her friends. His masculine scent, a mix of citrus and soap, teased her nostrils and sent arousal zinging through her veins. She gave him a teasing look and whispered in his ear, "I'm hoping for more later."

He grinned and took her hand. "I can't wait to meet your friends."

She pointed to them clockwise around the room. "That's Brianne Hart. She's the one I told you about that does book covers and is married to the doctor. That's Sara Jameson. She's a teacher and married to two men, and that's her new son, Jonah, sleeping. Remember, I told you she travels back and forth from Illinois? This is Lisa Hart. She's a sculptor, and her husband is a local attorney. And of course, on the webcam is newlywed Noelle Hunter. She lives in Montana now with her new family on a ranch. That's everybody. Everybody, this is Detective Ian Taggert. He recently moved next door. He's a cop and grills a great steak."

Ian looked shell-shocked. She didn't think meeting a few women who liked to read naughty books, drink martinis, and eat chocolate would freak him out, but she saw him swallow hard before speaking.

"It's nice to meet you, ladies. I don't mean to interrupt. I just stopped by to get a package that Tori was kind enough to accept for me." He turned on his heel and headed toward her front door. "Is the package in the foyer?"

Tori frowned and followed him. "Yes." She grabbed his arm when they exited the living room, and gave him an encouraging smile. "Don't be self-conscious, okay? My friends are really nice people. They're going to love you."

Ian exhaled and shook his head. "Sorry. If they're friends of yours, of course they're nice people. Listen, I'm just in a weird mood today. This case is making me a little crazy."

Ian was working the case of a serial rapist who liked to attack women in dark parking lots and alleys. So far, no one had been able to identify him other than average height and build with short brown hair. It was a description fitting half the men in the Tampa Bay area.

She placed her hand on his chest. "It's okay. I know this case is important. Will I see you later?"

Ian glanced back at the living room, and his expression was troubled. "If you still want to see me later, yes, come over and I'll fix dinner."

Tori frowned. "Why wouldn't I want to see you?"

He picked up his package and headed to the door. "Maybe you're tired of me?"

Tori felt a sharp pain in the vicinity of her heart. "Or maybe you're tired of me?"

Ian muttered an expletive under his breath. "No. I love being with you. I just—Listen, we need to talk when you come over tonight, okay? There's something important I need to tell you." He nervously glanced back at the living room full of women.

Tori watched as Ian left. Something was going on, and it had something to do with her best friends in all the world. She walked back into the living room and crossed her arms over her chest, tapping her foot on the polished bamboo flooring.

"Okay, which one of you wants to tell me something?"

The room was quiet, and then Lisa raised her hand. "Shit, Tori. I guess I do."

Sara looked aghast. "Oh my God, did you sleep with Tori's boyfriend?"

It was Lisa's turn to look shocked. "Fuck, no. I'm a happily married woman. I know him, that's all. Although, I didn't know his real name."

Tori sat down in the armchair feeling faint. "His real name? Son of a fucking bitch, Lisa, how do you know Ian?"

Pictures of a secret wife and kids were pounding Tori's brain. If Ian had a secret family she was going to kick his ass from here to

Sarasota.

Lisa sipped at her Cosmo, her cheeks pink. "I'm happy to tell you, Tori, but I think I should tell you alone. You may, or may not, want everyone to hear this."

The other women groaned. Brianne pursed her lips. "We're all friends here. You and I even trained Noelle to be a sub for Cam."

"And thanks for telling me all of you were in the BDSM lifestyle," Tori said. "I had to find out by accident when Noelle slipped and talked about her Master. Apparently, I was the only one who didn't know."

Sara rubbed her son's back to soothe him when he started to fuss in his sleep. "Technically, we're not in the lifestyle. We just play at it when we're in the mood." She giggled. "My boys love their games."

"Details." Tori waved her hand. "But I do want to hear this. Perhaps you're right I should hear it alone first. Am I going to faint or anything?"

Lisa rolled her eyes. "Are you a fainter?" She pushed Tori's martini closer to her. "Just in case."

Brianne stood up. "Well, I for one could do with some air. Sara and Noelle, what do you say we go sit on the patio for awhile? It's a beautiful day."

Noelle laughed. "I don't have much choice, Bri. I go where the laptop goes."

Her friends went outside, taking the laptop and webcam with them. Tori turned to Lisa. "Talk."

Lisa fidgeted a bit in her chair, clearly uncomfortable with the topic. "I know him from play parties. He's in the lifestyle, Tori. A regular, although I haven't seen him at any parties in a few months, come to think of it."

Tori let Lisa's words sink in. For some reason, she wasn't totally shocked. At this point in her life, very little shocked her anymore. "Dom, I assume?"

Lisa nodded. "Very Dom. He's known as the Devil Dom, which is why I didn't know his real name."

Tori slumped in her chair. "Devil Dom? Holy shit. Is he some kind of sadist?"

Lisa shook her head. "Not that I know of. He was dubbed the Devil Dom by a few subs, and it stuck. Apparently, his style is what they termed 'sexy as sin.' He's extremely dominant. All business when he's in a scene. Doesn't tolerate bratty subs and is known for punishing the least little infraction. To be fair, he doesn't set a sub up to fail like some Doms do. He's just strict and exacting. He's also known as one of the best Doms in the area. He's all about being safe, sane, and consensual. Subs are dying to be trained by him, but he's never been interested in taking on a full-time sub. I don't ever think I've seen him with the same sub more than a few times."

More good news. Her seemingly perfect boyfriend was a Dominant and maybe a player.

"It just gets better and better, Lisa. Is there anything else I should know? Is he the leader of the Hells Angels, too? Or maybe he's like 007 and is a secret agent for the government, with a license to kill?"

More like a license to thrill.

Now she understood why he said what he said. He had figured Lisa would tell on him, and he wasn't sure Tori would want to see him again.

"Nothing else I know of. Conor has talked to him quite a bit. Says he's a good guy."

"You've never talked to him?"

Lisa giggled. "An owned submissive doesn't get to chat with another Dom very often. Usually, I've been commanded not to speak unless Conor speaks to me. I get to chat with the subs, but Doms not so much." Lisa sipped her martini. "Besides, with Conor's schedule lately, we go and do a scene and leave. We don't stay and socialize much anymore. Not like before we had kids." Lisa sighed. "Conor works all the time. I think he loves his job more than me."

"I'm sure that's not true. Conor adores you." Tori twirled the base of her glass and chewed on her lip. She wasn't upset Ian was a Dom. Far from it. The idea of being dominated by someone who knew what he was doing had always been an arousing one for her. She'd wanted someone adventurous, and anyone with a nickname like the Devil Dom, probably had adventure in spades.

No, it was the fact he had been hiding it. Was he ever going to tell her, or had he pegged her as his vanilla girlfriend who wouldn't know when he went to parties to get his freak on? Did she appear to be boring and rigid?

If he's going to get his freak on with anyone, it's damn well going to be me.

She reached for a chocolate from the gold box on the table and gave Lisa a serene smile. "Thank you for telling me. I know you didn't want to, but now that I know I can talk to him about it."

"Are you going to kill him?"

Tori bit into the dark chocolate truffle, letting the bittersweet confection melt on her tongue. "No. I'm going to give him a chance to explain. But the explanation better be damn good."

"If it is good? What then?"

Tori popped the rest of the truffle in her mouth with a grin. "Then you and Brianne will have another submissive to train."

"If it isn't a good explanation?"

"Ian Taggert is history."

* * * *

Ian wasn't sure why he was getting ready to grill hamburgers for dinner. He also wasn't sure why he had taken a shower and shaved after work. The chances of Tori ever speaking to him again were remote. Her friend Lisa was surely going to tell her his dirty little secret. Their relationship was over.

When he'd met Tori three months ago, after moving into his new house, he'd been instantly attracted. More attracted than he could ever remember being, in fact. Her long dark hair and soft green eyes were gorgeous, and her tan-and-toned body made his fingers itch to explore her curves. She was in shape but not a stick figure. She was all woman, and she made him feel all man.

She was smart, funny, talented, and successful. She was the author of a bestselling series of children's books. She wasn't looking for a meal ticket or someone to take care of her. She stood on her own two feet. It was a characteristic Ian admired. Despite his dominant tendencies, he liked a woman who could take care of herself. He wasn't looking for a doormat.

Which was pretty much all he had found in the last several years. Either the woman in question was simply playing at the lifestyle and not really submissive, or they were submissive to the point they wanted him to make every decision of their day, including what to eat and when to take a shower. Neither the former nor the latter was his style.

He hadn't really had a plan when he'd asked Tori out. She hadn't seemed all that submissive, so in retrospect it had probably been a bad idea. Dammit, he couldn't help himself. The more time he spent with her, the more he wanted to be with her. After two months of telling himself to leave her alone, he couldn't ignore his feelings any longer. In the last three weeks, he had been coming to terms with the fact that his life as a Dominant was over.

If Tori didn't have any interest in the lifestyle, and he was pretty sure she didn't, then he was going to have to give up something. Giving up Tori seemed incomprehensible. She was the kind of woman he'd been looking for since his divorce five years ago. It was just his tough luck she wasn't submissive. He was sure he could get used to a life of vanilla sex. After all, sex was good no matter what, right?

"Are you making hamburgers for dinner?"

Ian whirled around and faced the woman who had filled his thoughts the last hour and half. The woman he thought would never speak to him again.

"Yes, it sounded good. Simple. Just hamburgers, chips, and I have some fruit salad left over from dinner last night."

Tori nodded. "Sounds good. Can I help?"

Ian was on his guard. Her expression was neutral. She didn't seem disgusted, but she was perhaps hiding it, not wanting to hurt his feelings. Tori had a soft, loving heart. He'd seen it when her twin sons had left for college a couple of months ago. The love between the three of them had been so real and genuine.

"Not really. The patties are made, and I can put them on the grill when we're ready to eat."

"I think we should have that talk first."

Ian sighed. He was about to get the heave-ho. He could only try and convince her he could live without the whole D/s thing. He was almost sure he could. She was worth the try.

"How about a glass of wine?" Ian motioned to the patio table, and Tori sat down while he poured her a glass of wine and refilled his own. He had a feeling he was going to need it.

He sat down in the chair next to hers and grabbed her hand. "There's something I need to tell you. I've been wanting to tell you but honestly haven't known how."

Tori put up her hand. "Lisa already told me. Unless, of course, you're referring to another secret you've kept from me?"

She sounded pissed off, and Ian couldn't blame her. As a Dom, he prized honesty. He hadn't been honest with her, and it was time to right the wrong.

"No, no other secrets. Fuck, Tori, I just didn't know how to tell you. I was afraid you'd never want to speak to me or see me again. I pictured you building a big ten-foot fence between our properties."

That brought a smile to her beautiful face. "Ten feet? I don't think the homeowner's association would be too thrilled about that."

"I'm sure if you told them the story, they'd give you a waiver."

Her expression was amused and, luckily, not angry. Ian had seen her moss-green eyes turn dark with passion and gold with happiness.

"Hmmm, you think I should tell them I've been dating this great guy but just found out from my best friend that he's been keeping a secret from me? He's a Dom in his private life and they call him the Devil."

Ian could feel the heat stain his cheeks. He'd always hated his nickname, given to him by a brat of a sub when he wouldn't continue training her. She didn't have a submissive bone in her body, and he wasn't going to waste his time. She'd eventually left the lifestyle but had left the legacy of the Devil Dom.

"It's a nickname. Not one I'm fond of, by the way." Ian scraped his hand down his face. Saying the words was harder than he had imagined. "Listen, I'm ready to give all that up. I'm sorry I kept it from you, but I was seriously nervous you would kick my ass to the curb. I like being a Dom. Hell, I love it. But I've been waiting years to meet a woman like you. You're someone I can see myself with in the future. I want to see where this relationship can go. If I have to give the other up for you, well, then I have to."

"If you have to? Sounds like you don't really want to, if you ask me."

Ian jumped to his feet. "If you're asking if I'd like to have it all, then the answer is yes. I'd like to have you as my submissive. Fuck, yes, Tori. But I'm not a stupid man. People don't always get what they want."

Tori nodded. "True. How come you never even broached the subject with me? Do I seem vanilla? Am I that boring you didn't even think to talk about it with me? See what I think?"

Shock shot through his body. She wanted him to discuss it with her? Was she open to submitting to him?

"You are not boring. Shit. And where did you learn the term 'vanilla'?"

Tori reached over to the purse she had tossed on a chair and pulled out her e-reader. She punched a few buttons and handed it to him.

"Look. Look at what our book club reads."

Ian paged through the titles in her e-reader in amazement. His woman was a BDSM-book addict. He didn't need to open most of the books to see what they were about. The titles were fairly descriptive.

"I guess you had a secret, too."

She rolled her eyes, and a touch of pink colored her cheeks. "I didn't think my reading material was a big deal until this afternoon." She reached across and laid her hand on his tanned arm. "I have an open mind, Ian." She gave a self-deprecating laugh. "I have no actual real-life experience having an open mind, sexually speaking, but I am open to us talking about this."

He put her e-reader back on the table. "How open-minded are you? Are you open-minded enough to discuss a Dominant-submissive relationship? Wow, I can't believe we're having this discussion. I thought you would be shocked and mortified. Think I was some kind of pervert."

He still couldn't believe she wasn't running a mile in the other direction. He hadn't had much luck in his personal life, and it seemed too good to be true she might want to explore his dark secret with him.

"I don't think you're a pervert. As you know, Lisa and Conor have a D/s relationship. The other women in the club do, also, although Sara says they only play at it when they're in the mood."

He nodded. "There's no right or wrong way. Some people live every minute of their lives that way, some people when they're in the mood, and everything in between."

Tori frowned. "Which are you?"

He took his time answering the question. He'd had several years to figure it out for himself, but explaining wasn't always easy. "I'm somewhere in between. I like being in charge in the bedroom. Period. No leeway there. The rest of the time, it's more complex. I want a woman who can be a partner to me. I don't want to have to control her every move and thought. But I do want to take care of her."

Tori sipped her wine. "What does take care of her mean?"

He lifted her hand and played with her delicate fingers, the nails cut short, as she was on her laptop all the time. "It means I want to order for her in restaurants. It means I want to make sure she's safe. I want to hear about her lousy day and make all the bad things better."

"What if I don't like what you order for me?"

Ian laughed. "Is that what you're worried about? We would discuss what you wanted, but when the waiter came to the table, I would order for you. How does that sound?"

Her expression was so serious and cute. "That would be okay. I'm a really picky eater."

"I know. I've learned that about you these last months."

He could see the wheels turning in her mind. He needed to find out what she was thinking about.

"You would want to be in charge? What if I didn't agree with something? What if you're being an asshole?"

They were getting down to the nitty-gritty. "Any man can be an asshole, sweetheart, even a Dom. I work hard at not being one, but Dom's make mistakes. The key is to acknowledge them and learn from them. If we didn't agree on something, we would talk about it. Just like other couples. The only difference is if I thought it was something that concerned your health, well-being, or safety, I would insist you follow my command. And I would punish you if you didn't obey me. As my submissive, you would agree that I was in charge of those three things."

He watched her closely as she processed his words. He'd chosen them carefully, for effect. She needed to know up front what this was about.

"What if I didn't like your punishment?"

Ian had to laugh. "Punishments aren't meant to be fun, honey. They're punishments. However, in a D/s relationship, we would agree what rules should be followed. You would agree to be punished for breaking them and that I will choose the method of punishment. You would have to trust that I will be just in meting out discipline."

Her eyebrow arched in question. "Just? From the man called the Devil Dom?"

He gave her his sternest Dom look. "I told you it was a nickname."

He hid his grin when her body language instantly responded to his dominance. Her eyes dropped and her pupils dilated. She might be submissive, after all.

He brought her fingers to his lips and kissed them softly. "And as a Dom who prizes honesty, I need to acknowledge and apologize for keeping this secret from you. Fear is not something I am comfortable with, Tori. I was instantly attracted to you and fought that attraction for some time before I succumbed. I told myself finding a partner was more important than being a Dom. I am truly sorry for keeping this from you, and I ask your forgiveness."

Chapter Two

She'd never had a man ask for forgiveness so sincerely. Ian was truly sorry for keeping his secret. She breathed a sigh of relief her judgment regarding him wasn't off. He was a good person. At this point, there was only one question left.

Do I want to be his submissive?

She wasn't sure she was ready for that question. She stalled by asking him something else.

"I do forgive you, Ian. I can understand why you did it now that you've explained. But I need to know. Is that why we haven't slept together? Do you not like having vanilla sex?"

Laughter rumbled from his chest, and a wide smile covered his face. "Honey, I love sex in all its forms. Do you imagine I would have you tied up every single night? I wish. Life gets in the way. We get busy at work, and we get tired. Sometimes, vanilla sex is all there's time for. We haven't had sex for two reasons. One, I knew it had been a long time for you. I didn't want to rush you into something you weren't ready for. Two, I was unsure myself. I wanted you but haven't had a totally vanilla relationship in years. Since the early years in my marriage, frankly."

"I'm confused then. Why were you concerned about living a vanilla life then?"

"As much as I like vanilla sex, and I do, I prefer to be dominant. I enjoy crafting a scene with a submissive. I wasn't sure I could live without it, but you were worth trying it for."

She looked deep into his beautiful blue eyes. He'd been courageous in trying to change his life. For her. She was deeply humbled. Her conversations with Lisa, Brianne, and Noelle had educated her as to how ingrained dominant and submissive tendencies were. He was willing to try, and that had to mean something.

So what the hell do I want?

She'd had vanilla and it was nice. She'd been reading BDSM stories and fantasizing for a long time now. In her fantasies, she was submitting to a hot, sexy Dom. Now she had one sitting right across from her, offering more than sex. He was offering her a shot at a relationship. She hadn't really been looking for anything serious. She was looking for a monogamous relationship, and he wasn't talking marriage, thank goodness.

She took a fortifying sip from her wine. "I think I might be submissive."

There, I said it.

He leaned back in his chair, and she felt his gaze on her face. "You might be. That may explain part of my strong attraction to you. You're an independent woman, and any submissive tendencies you may have are not overt. They're deep inside. I've seen a few signs today, but they were fleeting. Are you saying you want to explore this possibility?"

She licked her suddenly dry lips. "Yes. I want to. With you."

Frustration crossed his face, and her heart fell. He didn't want her. "Tori, I've fantasized about dominating you from practically the moment I met you. If we do this and it doesn't work out...our relationship will, in all probability, be over. We can't go back in time and be vanilla as if your submission never happened. You can't un-ring a bell."

She breathed a little easier. He did want her, but he was as scared as she was. "It's a risk either way. If I don't try this, our vanilla relationship might not work out either. Logic, and my gut, tell me the odds wouldn't be in our favor. You are who you are. If we have any chance, we need to explore a Dominant-submissive relationship."

He stood up and refilled her glass. He was smiling and shaking his head. "Brave, aren't you, honey? You're probably right. You seem to be right all the time, anyway. It's a risk either way. I can certainly give you an introduction to the lifestyle if you're willing. I'll go inside and get the hamburgers for the grill and the paperwork for you."

Tori blinked. "I have to fill out an application to submit to you?"

He laughed so hard the neighbors probably heard it. She scowled at his amusement. She was trying to be serious here.

"No, honey. No application. But this is a questionnaire that will give me a window into your likes, dislikes, fantasies, and so forth. It will help me figure out how to proceed."

"Don't you know what to do?" She was surprised. Lisa said he had a great deal of experience.

"Every submissive has to be treated individually. There's no prescription for training a sub. I don't want to treat you like anyone else." He leaned down and pressed his lips to hers, pulling her up against him. The heat from his body set hers aflame. She pressed herself closer as his tongue explored her mouth. She ran her hands down his muscular back and gave herself up to her senses. She could smell the tang of his soap, taste the wine on his tongue, feel the beat of his heart, and hear the roar of blood in her ears. He lifted his head all too soon. "You're special. I'm going to treat you like the special woman, and submissive, you are."

Ian turned and went in the house, leaving her with her jumbled thoughts. He was a special man, and she wanted to be with him so bad she ached with it. Time would tell how submissive, and adventurous, she really was. She only knew she was finally getting the chance to find out.

* * * *

Tori sat at her kitchen table and bit into the dark-chocolate brownie she would be working off in the gym tomorrow. When Carl had passed away, she'd realized she'd let herself go over the years.

She had been about sixty pounds overweight and never bothered with makeup or styling her hair. She'd cast a critical eye at her life and found it wanting. She'd withdrawn from life when taking care of Carl during those last few years. The start of her new life was when she had tentatively walked into her neighborhood gym and signed a year contract. Within months her two sons were cheering her on. It felt good to have them be proud of her. Now she wanted to be proud of herself. It didn't mean, however, she couldn't have a damn brownie every now and then.

She picked up the pen and blew out a breath. The paperwork Ian had asked her to fill out was incredibly personal and more than a little embarrassing. It was some small comfort she was filling it out in the privacy of her own home. Eventually, he was going to read it, and it was like stripping herself bare for him, a thought which made her groan. She had no doubt she would be stripping bare for him, and soon. There wasn't much chance of getting to keep her clothes on while they were having sex.

The soft chimes of her cell phone gave her the excuse she was looking for to take a break. She smiled when she saw the caller, and pressed the accept button.

"Hey, Lisa. What's up?"

"I called to see how your talk with the Devil, shit, I mean Ian, went. Did you work everything out?"

"We did. He was willing to give up being a Dominant to pursue a relationship with me."

There was silence on the other end of the phone for a long moment. "Holy crap, that's big. He must really be attracted to you. He's really going to give up the lifestyle for you? That can't be easy for him. I don't think Conor and I could go vanilla after all these years."

"He's not going vanilla. I agreed to try submitting to him."

Lisa chuckled. "Good for you. I always knew you had it in you. I think you'll love it, but then I'm biased. I never feel more free than when I'm submitting to Conor."

"I want to feel that way, too. But first I have to fill out all this paperwork. He gave me homework, Lisa. I have a five-page questionnaire to fill out. Then, I am also to troll the internet looking for things I find intriguing and things I find disgusting. God, what's next? A pop quiz?"

"Better study up, girlfriend. You'll get more than a detention if you disobey the Devil Dom. You'll get your ass warmed up, I'll bet."

Tori's pussy dripped honey at the thought of being bent over Ian's muscular thighs with his firm hand spanking her bottom. It was an erotic and naughty picture, and it made her even more sure of her decision to try this. She wanted to explore this submissive stuff completely.

"The questions are very personal. He's asking questions about whether I would consider anal play and anal sex."

"Keep an open mind. I love anal play and anal sex. I assume you and Carl never did that?"

"Never. He didn't express an interest and neither did I. In fact, I never gave it much thought until we started reading erotic books. I'll mark it a 'maybe.' I'm supposed to mark each item 'yes,' 'no,' or 'maybe.'"

"He's figuring out your hard limits. You can tell a good Dom when he really tries to find out your needs. You're lucky, Tori. There are so many assholes out there just pretending to be Doms."

"I told you I felt like I won the lottery. Shit, I need to finish this homework. I'm supposed to put this all in an envelope and put it on his patio by noon tomorrow. I'm guessing this is my first chance to obey him."

"I don't want to be the reason you get punished. Finish your homework and I'll talk to you tomorrow. Listen, have fun with this. Enjoy it. This is an exciting time for you."

Tori said goodnight and hung up the phone, tapping the pen against her chin. There was a part of her wanting to disobey this first directive just to see what he'd do, but her logic overruled the notion. There was no doubt he was going to have ample opportunities to punish her, and she had a feeling she was going to enjoy it.

* * * *

"Ian, I think you need to see this." Detective Tim Mills was Ian's sometime partner. They would work cases together on occasion, although Ian preferred to work alone. Tim was great with victims and perps alike. He had a way with people that Ian admired. Tim was a nice guy and was pleasant to be around, although he seemed to want recognition for every arrest, major or minor. Ian put it down to ambition and didn't pay it much attention.

"Sure, Tim. What's up?" Ian hoped it wasn't something to keep him working late tonight. After last night's conversation with Tori, Ian was anxious to get home and see if she completed her homework assignment. He'd barely slept last night, his body buzzing with arousal. He had one chance with Tori to show her a D/s lifestyle didn't mean the end of her independence, and he wasn't going to screw it up. He wanted to show her the lifestyle was about more than bondage and floggings, although it was certainly a fun part. It was about two people caring for each other, being honest, and communicating their needs.

"The mail room found this in today's mail. It was addressed to you. Luckily, they're smart and they called in the forensic guys immediately."

Tim placed a plastic bag on the desk. Inside was a letter and an envelope with a local postmark. Ian picked it up, and as he read his blood ran cold. He looked up at Tim, who was perched on the edge of the desk.

"This is from The Boyfriend. He knows things we haven't released to the press."

They'd kept the detail about a rose being left at each of the crime scenes a secret. The person who wrote this was aware of it.

"Was forensics able to get anything? Fingerprints or DNA?"

Tim shrugged. "No fingerprints. They swabbed for DNA, but it will take weeks for it to come back. You know the drill. It's not like on television."

Ian knew only too well. Everyone thought DNA came back in hours and forensic teams worked every crime scene, even small robberies.

"Tampa postmark. The guy could be local."

Tim stood up and looked out the window. "Maybe. There are an awful lot of little communities around here. He could have driven in from any one of them and mailed that letter."

Ian shook his head in frustration. "I don't like this. The guy is taunting us now. Look at what he says."

So far, I've defiled four women. I'll continue until you catch me. I have dozens of roses to hand out to deserving girls. I'm closer than you think. She's next.

Tim handed him another plastic bag with a photo in it. "This is the picture he sent. Do you know her? Is that why he sent it to you?"

Ian studied every detail of the picture, his stomach tightening. The guy was stalking the women ahead of time. "No. I wish to hell I did. He probably sent it to me since I was on the news the other night. That damn reporter wouldn't leave me alone. What are we doing to track her down?"

"We've got the FBI doing some facial recognition, but this picture sucks. He gave us just enough information to frustrate us. There's not a whole hell of a lot we can do. We sure as hell can't broadcast this out on the evening news and tell the world this is the next victim. Shit, there'd be panic in the streets. Anyone who even slightly resembled this woman would be hysterical."

"Are they looking at the details in the photo for any clues? Signs, streets, anything?"

"Forensics is on it, but they think he photoshopped her into this background. This guy is smart."

"Criminals aren't usually very bright. He's seen one too many episodes of *CSI*, that's all. We'll get him."

"This one is smart. Damn smart. He's making us cops look like amateurs."

Ian stood up and paced his office. This case was maddening. "It sounds like he's saying he's finding girls in his own neighborhood. Maybe he knows the victims in some way."

Tim turned toward the bulletin board and pointed. "Four victims, four different areas of Tampa. South Tampa, New Tampa, downtown, and the USF area. All spread out. Not sure how he would know them. Maybe he worked with them or went to school with them?"

Ian grabbed his coffee cup and absently took a sip, almost spitting it out in disgust. The coffee was ice cold. How long had he been in his office looking through police reports to find the one clue that would give them an opening?

He slammed down the cup with a grimace. "We're still getting the standard questions answered. Their questionnaires should have all we need to see if there are any similarities. Hairdressers, restaurants, cleaning services, or whatever. If there are any commonalities, we'll find it."

Tim grinned. "And when we do, we'll get him."

Ian headed to the coffee machine. "We need to catch this guy. He's going to escalate, and someone is going to get killed. I won't let it happen on my watch."

Chapter Three

Tori wriggled her toes and stretched her legs with a yawn. It had been a long day. She'd cleaned the house, done two loads of laundry, and worked on the new book in her Tucker the Bear series. Ian had shown up at her door after work as tired as she was. They'd ordered a pizza and were now watching *American Pickers*.

"That was a big yawn, young lady. Rough day?"

She snuggled closer to his warm body and delicately sniffed the air. "Do you smell that? It's furniture polish and disinfectant. I cleaned the house from top to bottom today. It's easier now that it's only me than when Aaron and Adam were here, but it's still a job. I need to move to a smaller house."

It was an idle threat. Her two sons were away at college but would be home at the holidays and during the summers. She needed every bit of space she had in this house and then some. It felt almost too small when her fully grown sons were home.

Ian pulled her onto his lap, nuzzling her neck and making her giggle. "No way, sweetheart. I love having you as a neighbor. I've never had a neighbor as gorgeous as you, and you don't have a loud stereo either."

"Or a broken truck parked in my front yard."

Ian had told her about his neighbors in his last house. They were nice people but had driven him crazy with their idiosyncrasies. He was thrilled to be out of a condo complex and into a single-family home.

Ian reached for the remote and muted the television. "I was hoping we could go over your homework tonight. Are you okay with that?"

Tori felt an immediate flush of heat run through her body. It had been embarrassing answering the questions, but it had also been arousing. She'd imagined them doing some of those things together. Her panties had been wet and her nipples tight and painful by the time she'd finished.

She nodded. "Okay. I guess we can do that."

He lifted her off his lap and went to grab the envelope he'd set on her kitchen counter. She tried to relax. She'd seen him bring the envelope, so she knew this was coming, but she couldn't suppress a moment of doubt. She wasn't sure what she would do if he wanted her to do something she really didn't want to do or was fearful of doing.

He pulled the papers from the envelope and started flipping through them. "I looked through this earlier. First of all, thank you for finishing them and following my instructions. I appreciate it." He gave her an approving smile, and she felt the glow of accomplishment. It pleased her that she had pleased him. It seemed silly but it was true.

"We're on the same wavelength, which is good news. Your hard limits match most of my own."

"You have limits?" She hadn't expected that.

"Of course. Doms have limits, too. I don't like to mete out harsh pain or anything which will leave a permanent mark. I don't want to make you bleed or burn your skin. I also don't do breath play."

She nodded vigorously. "That's good. Really good."

He turned to the third page. "I see you have a hard limit on humiliation of any kind. Let's talk about this one. When you think about humiliation, are you thinking about it in a verbal sense or a physical sense?"

Tori frowned. "I'm not sure what you mean. Are you talking about calling me names?"

"Yes. Some subs like it when a Dom calls them 'slut,' 'whore,' or something like that. They like it when the Dom tells them they're only good for one thing."

She didn't like the sound of any of that. "I don't want to be called names. That just seems mean, not arousing."

"Fair enough. Let's talk about physical. Would you consider kneeling humiliation?"

"No. I expected to kneel for you." She'd fantasized about it, if the truth be known.

"How about if I spanked you and put you in the corner to think about your transgressions?"

"I guess it would be okay," Tori said slowly. The spanking idea turned her on. Being put in the corner was neutral. It didn't arouse her, but it didn't turn her off either. It was a harmless activity.

"You would be okay if I did that at a play party, in a room full of people? Would you kneel, kiss my feet, and then take your punishment?"

Tori wanted to say no, but her body had other ideas. The image of kneeling, kissing his shoes reverently, and then being punished had sent honey dripping from her pussy. She fidgeted in her seat as her cunt clenched in response.

"In front of other people? Would I be naked?"

"Yes. Although, if it helps, the other slaves would no doubt be naked, or near it, also."

It didn't really help. She was naturally modest. He put the papers down. "Would you consider it humiliating to be naked in a room full of people? Would you be humiliated to be gagged and bound in front of others?"

Tori knew Lisa and Conor went to play parties. Brianne and Nate, also. Nudity there was probably no big deal.

"I'm naturally modest. I know this will sound strange, but I'm more worried about being naked in front of people than I am about doing things of a sexual nature in front of them. Crazy, I know."

Ian stroked his chin. "Are you willing to work on your modesty?"

She nodded. "Yes. I know it's something I'm going to have to get over."

"Good. Let's start now. Take off all your clothes."

Huh?

"Take off your clothes, Tori." His voice had deepened, and she felt herself respond instantly. A shiver went down her spine, and more cream dripped from her cunt. His voice compelled her to obey. She popped open the button on her shorts and pulled down the zipper. She shed her shorts quickly and tugged her shirt over her head. All that was left were her bra and panties. She felt a blush crawl up her chest and face. He's seen her in a bikini, so she wasn't sure why she was so shy. Maybe it was the heat in his eyes as they roamed over her scantily clad form. He looked like he wanted to make love to her.

Isn't that what you want?

Her hands trembled slightly as she reached for the butterfly clip between her breasts. She paused for a moment and glanced up at him. He sat quietly, waiting. He didn't say a word but simply watched her with a calm, controlled expression. He expected her to obey. She swallowed and flicked open the clasp, pushing the bra down her arms and onto the coffee table before she lost her nerve. She pulled her panties down her legs just as quickly, afraid to meet his eyes.

Finally, she was completely nude. She was shaking with the effort of sitting there and not covering herself. She hadn't been naked with another man since her late husband. It was terrifying.

"Stand up, Tori."

She didn't think she'd heard him correctly. He placed his fingers under her chin and made her look into his eyes. His expression was stern. "I commanded you to stand. I expect my orders to be complied with immediately. I do not want to have to repeat myself over and over. This is twice you have hesitated to obey me. Do you want to call an end to your submission?"

Tori shook her head. She absolutely did not. "No, Ian. I want to do this. I really do."

"I do not tolerate disobedience. You'll receive six. On the bare."

Before she could ask him what she was getting six of, he was pulling her down over his knees. It became clear she was going to be spanked. Her nipples tightened to hard buds, and the honey dripped down her thighs. How many times had she fantasized about being draped over the hard thighs of a sexy man and spanked on her bottom? Too many to count. It was about to come true.

The first smack on her bottom shocked her. It wasn't a love pat. His rough hand had come down on her ass cheek hard. She jumped with surprise, and one of her hands flew back instinctively to protect herself. He chuckled and caught her wrist, pressing it into the small of her back and using his elbow on her upper back to push her torso lower so her ass thrust up in invitation.

She almost stopped him, but then the heat from her bottom was traveling to her pussy and clit and it was becoming a delicious sensation. She wanted to savor it, but his hand came down again on the other cheek. She was more prepared this time and waited for the pleasure to follow the pain. Four more strikes on her tender flesh followed. He spanked her with measured, slow strokes, pausing in between long enough for her to feel the heat and then the arousal. The spanking was over too soon. She was dripping wet by the time he was done. He lifted her from his lap and stood her on her feet.

"Good girl. You did well. Now, into the corner to think about why you were punished."

Despite the fact they'd discussed being put in a corner not ten minutes prior, she was still surprised when he said it. He was really going to put her in a corner like a naughty child?

Once again, he simply waited for her compliance. He was pointing to a corner of the living room, and she sighed and headed for it. As far as punishments went, it was pretty minor and quite harmless. She'd put her twins in the corner a few times when they were small and she'd been at her wit's end.

He pressed her nose into the corner and brought her hands behind her back.

"No rubbing your sore bottom. Keep your hands here. Spread your legs a little."

She pushed her legs apart, but apparently it wasn't enough. He tapped on the inside of her feet lightly and she spread them a few more inches.

"Good. You stay there until I come back for you. Don't turn around. I want you to think about why you were punished and how you might correct your behavior."

She heard him turn around and head into the kitchen. She stood there waiting, with a burning bottom, and couldn't stop her mind from wandering to how she'd ended up there. She'd hesitated to obey him. Considering it had been in the first half hour of submitting to his dominance it wasn't a shock. What was a shock was that he wasn't going to cut her any damn slack. Lisa had been right. He was exacting and strict and she was going to have to learn to obey him.

He hadn't ordered her to do anything radical. He'd asked her to take off her clothes, something she'd been anxious to do with him. In the right setting, of course, with his clothes coming off, too. Yes, she'd been embarrassed, but the more she thought about it, it had more to do with the fact he'd still been dressed.

That's submission.

She now also knew why she was standing in a corner. He was giving her the opportunity to figure it out for herself. Now she had, she was ready to be let out. She fidgeted on her feet, chafing at the restriction. This must be the punishment part.

He'd come back into the living room and unmuted the television. She waited for what seemed like ages, but was probably only five or ten minutes, before he muted it again and placed his hand on her shoulder. Her senses were assailed with his warmth and the manly scent from his body. She felt her honey drip down her thighs.

"You may turn around, Tori."

* * * *

Tori's eyes were downcast, and her body language spoke of a sub who was sorry for misbehaving. His cock twitched in his pants and pressed hard against his zipper. He'd grown used to having a hard-on when Tori was around, but it had passed the painful point when her gorgeous body had been draped over his knees in supplication. Her round bottom was perfect for spanking, and he'd enjoyed every minute of initiating her into the pleasures of corporal punishment. He knew she'd enjoyed it, too. She'd left a puddle of cream on his thighs.

"Tori, please tell me why you were punished. And look me in the eyes when you do."

He kept his voice even and firm despite his arousal. His pretty new sub raised her eyes and bit her bottom lip. "I didn't obey you. I made you repeat your commands. I'm sorry, uh, Sir, or Master. I'm not really sure how you wish me to address you."

"In my opinion, and many would disagree with me, Sir is a title for when you are scening with a Dominant but don't belong to him specifically. Do you belong to me, Tori? Are we a couple?"

She nodded, her eyes wide.

"Then you will address me as Master or Master Ian when we are in a scene or we are in Dominant-submissive mode. We are in such mode now. You will come to recognize this as we work together. Now, you are correct as to why you were punished. Have you thought about how to correct your behavior?"

She pressed her lips together, her cheeks a lovely pink color. Tori was a beautiful woman in the prime of her life. He knew she'd had her sons at the tender age of eighteen, so despite being an empty nester, she was only thirty-six. He was one year younger and tired of twenty-something subs wanting him to train them but unable to stop texting long enough to be restrained. Tori was smart and classy, and he was damn lucky to have found her.

"I hesitated to obey because you were still dressed. I realize this is part of submission, and your request was not unreasonable. I need to learn to obey you and trust you without overthinking things."

He nodded, pleased she had worked out why she had disobeyed. Once again, it spoke of her emotional maturity and gave him hope their relationship would work. He'd never met a submissive with such introspection. It was a gift and one he would carefully reward and cultivate.

"I'm very pleased, Tori. Shall we continue our discussion and look through your paperwork?"

He threw a large cushion on the floor next to the couch. "You can sit here. A submissive generally sits at the feet of her Dominant."

To his surprise, Tori didn't hesitate. She curled up on the pillow with a nervous smile. He stroked her hair and rubbed her shoulders, bringing a sigh from her full lips. He wanted to give her positive reinforcement for obeying his command without question.

"You need a safeword. Do you have any preference?"

"No, Master Ian."

"We'll use 'red' and 'yellow' then. They're commonly used and easy to remember. If you need everything to stop, you use 'red.' If you need me to slow down, go easier, or catch your breath, you use 'yellow.' From time to time, I may check in on you and ask you where you are. You respond with 'red,' 'yellow,' or 'green.' Eventually, as we get to know one another, I won't need to check in very often, but at the beginning, I'll check in with you quite a bit." He picked up the papers from the coffee table. "I see you have 'yes' for anal play and 'maybe' for anal sex. Have you ever had anal sex?"

She was a brighter shade of pink now. "Um, no, Master. I've never done anything…like that."

"We'll go slow then." He flipped to the last page. "I see in the items on the internet you found interesting was some wax play. Is this something you would like for us to explore at some point?"

He didn't imagine her breathing rate increased and her eyes got brighter. Tori was turned-on.

"Yes, Master."

"You also have 'yes' on wrist and ankle bondage, gags, blindfolds, cock sucking, nipple clamps, paddling and flogging. Are those a solid 'yes'?"

She licked her lips. "Yes, Master." Tori's voice was barely above a whisper.

"Are you sure? We can change these to 'maybe.'"

She straightened her shoulders and firmed her chin. "No, Master. They're a solid 'yes.'"

Brave sub.

"You have 'maybe' for whipping with a single-tail. Good answer. It's good to be cautious about certain things. I'm an expert with one, but we'll push that to the future and see how things go. I'm good if it's something you don't want to do at all."

She was looking down now, and as much as he enjoyed her submissive posture he wanted to see her eyes darken with passion. He wanted to see her come. He lifted her chin with his fingers.

"Just a few more rules. When we are in a scene, you will not speak without permission or unless asked a direct question by myself. When we are in Dominant-submissive mode you may speak to me but no one else without permission. You are not to touch yourself in a pleasurable way, and you are not to come without permission. Ever. All pleasure comes solely from me from this moment forward. Do you understand, Tori?"

Her beautiful green eyes widened in dismay. However, she hesitated only a moment. "Yes, Master."

She'd been celibate for a long time, and with her habit of reading erotic books, he imagined she probably had a few toys in the nightstand. He'd assumed she'd masturbated regularly. No woman as sensuous as Tori could have gone four and a half years without an orgasm.

"I want you to go into your bedroom and bring me all of your sex toys. No exceptions. They belong to me as of now."

He had to hide his smile at her expression of amazement. He kept his features stern. There would be time for tenderness, but this wasn't the moment.

She scuttled into her bedroom and he heard the frantic opening and closing of drawers. He cleared his throat a few times to swallow his laughter. Tori was indeed a submissive woman, in the bedroom at least. So far, he'd punished her, set her at his feet, and commanded her to turn over all pleasure into his hands. A non-submissive woman would have had his nuts in a vise by now.

She returned, her face a fiery red and her arms full. She placed on the floor a bright purple vibrator with rabbit ears for clit stimulation, two vibrating eggs, and a bottle of lube.

He nodded. "Excellent. I'm very pleased and proud of you tonight, Tori. Time for your reward. Lay back on the pillow and spread your legs."

* * * *

She couldn't wait to find out what her reward might be. She'd been mortified to bring out her small collection of sex toys, but he'd barely blinked. What she thought of as deeply embarrassing, he apparently looked upon as merely ho-hum. Now she was being rewarded for her bravery and obedience, after being punished a short time ago. It was exciting, scary, and very arousing.

She lay on her back, spreading her legs. She knew he could see her pussy wet with her own juices. She couldn't remember the last time she'd been this turned on. So far, this submission stuff was pretty hot. Even now, Ian's expression was stern, but his eyes were tender and kind. She wasn't afraid in the least. It was arousing when he was strict, but she trusted him to be fair.

He let his gaze roam over her body, and then his finger drew a line from the hollow at her throat all the way down her torso to her pussy.

"My new property is beautiful, very sexy." He ran his hands up her belly and cupped her breasts, sending tingles of pleasure straight to her pussy and clit. "Your skin is golden and soft to the touch." He leaned down and pressed a kiss right above her belly button. "And your scent is delicious, a mix of vanilla and the musk from your arousal. It makes your Master's cock ache."

Her eyes were drawn to his crotch, and her mouth watered in anticipation. His shorts were tented, and his cock outlined against his zipper. His proportions looked generous and her pussy clenched, needing to be filled.

"Your breasts are the perfect size. They overflow my hands and will be gorgeous clamped or bound." His hands, callused from yard work, stroked her skin and plucked at her already painfully hard nipples. She panted as her arousal grew, and she reached for him to bring him down on top of her. He caught her hands in midair.

"Uh uh, my slave. You stay still while I explore. Hold onto the pillow under your head tightly. Nothing will happen unless I decide it's going to happen. You have no choices to make, no decisions to think about. Close your eyes and feel. All you need to do is feel."

She whimpered but did as he asked, grabbing the pillow and closing her eyes. She willed her body to relax as his fingers glided across every inch of her skin from her head to her toes. She wasn't used to not having something expected of her. It was a little frightening. What if she was supposed to be doing something and she wasn't doing it?

Her eyes popped open.

"I told you to close your eyes, slave. Why have you opened them?"

She gripped the pillow a little tighter. "I'm afraid."

He pulled his hands away and she felt bereft. His expression was all concern. "Do you need to use your safeword? What are you afraid of, sweetness?"

"I'm afraid I'm supposed to be doing something and I'm not doing it."

It sounded ridiculous when she said it, but he didn't laugh. He nodded as if she'd said something wise and enlightening.

"Completely natural, Tori. You've been in charge for years, haven't you? Everything was yours to do or decide. Even when your husband was ill, things fell to you. Then raising your sons alone, making a career for yourself, paying bills, everything. With your Master, you can let go of all that. I'll worry about everything for you. You don't have any responsibilities except to obey me. That's it. If I haven't told you to do something then you are doing exactly what you need to do. Relax and just be."

She laughed. "I don't remember the last time I did that. I'm in charge twenty-four-seven."

His finger dipped into her pussy and circled her clit, drawing a moan from her. "Then we'll make a memory tonight. Close your eyes, my slave, and let your mind run free."

She did as he bade and tried to let her thoughts wander. She didn't want to think about looming deadlines or unwashed dishes. She wanted to concentrate on his amazing hands. Hands which were doing wonderful things to her body. He pressed two fingers inside of her and she tightened on them, wanting more. He finger fucked her slowly, rubbing on her sweet spot and brushing his thumb against her swollen clit. She licked her lips and groaned, close to release.

"My new pussy is very tight. It's going to feel wonderful when I'm deep inside it, fucking it hard, and riding it to orgasm. Tighten on my fingers again, slave."

She tightened her muscles just as his tongue licked her clit. She almost came off the floor, the feeling like electricity shooting through her veins.

"Oh! Oh, Ian!"

She could feel his warm breath on her pussy. "That's 'Master' to you, little slave. Say it for me."

She panted as he lapped at her pussy and clit. "Master! Oh, Master!"

"Good girl. I want you to come for me now. Come good and hard for your Master."

His mouth closed over her clit and his fingers rubbed the swollen spot deep inside her. He sucked and licked, and her body exploded into thousands of pieces. Multi-colored lights danced on her eyelids, and she tried to catch her breath as the ecstasy ripped through her. He licked up all her cream as she came down to earth, feeling cared for and sated. He lay down next to her and pulled her into his arms.

"Whenever we are together, my slave, afterward we will have aftercare. It's our time to be close and intimate, just the two of us. It's my time to show you how proud I am of you and to care for you in any way you need to be cared for. We'll cuddle and talk, and we'll do this for as long as you need it. Don't try and cut this time short."

It felt too wonderful to rush through. His hard body was pressed close to hers, and he was stroking her hair, telling her how sexy and beautiful she was. She never wanted it to end. He pressed his lips to hers in a soft-but-hot kiss, letting his tongue trace the outline of her mouth.

She giggled when his teeth nibbled at her lower lip. "What about you, Master?"

He snuggled her, letting her feel the heat of his body. She could clearly feel the outline of his very hard and swollen cock.

"What about me, Tori?"

She pressed into him, rubbing against the bulge in his shorts. "Can't I take care of you?"

"Have I given you a command to take care of me?"

He hadn't. "No. I mean, no, Master."

He rubbed his chin on the top of her head. "Then it's nothing you need to concern yourself with. If I wanted you to serve me in some way, I would command you to do so."

"Okay." She pulled back and gave him a look of disbelief. "Aren't you uncomfortable?"

He smiled. "Very. But this is your first night. Let's take this submission thing a step at a time."

She ran her hands down his flat stomach and over the bulge in his pants, hearing his breath make a hissing sound when she caressed the ridge. He moved her hands back to his chest.

"No, Tori. You won't be getting fucked tonight. We're going to save that for another time. Now forget about my cock. I want to talk about how you felt tonight. What you liked. What surprised you."

With his hard dick pressed so closely it was going to be very difficult to forget, but she'd try. She concentrated on his question instead.

"I liked pretty much everything, although being put in the corner was surprising. I didn't really mind it, I was just surprised."

"I find time for contemplation helps a submissive come to terms with punishment and reward."

"I liked my reward." She gave him a grin and rubbed his chest.

"I liked it, too. I'm going to get you some water. You need to stay hydrated. I take my job as your Dom very seriously, and taking care of your health is important. Don't move, pretty slave. I'll be right back so we can talk more."

He levered up from the pillow and padded on bare feet into the kitchen. She wouldn't go anywhere. She was happy and content to follow Master Ian's orders. She just hoped his next orders would involve removing his pants.

And his shirt. And his underwear.

She really needed to convince him she was ready to make love with him. She wanted it more than ever. She couldn't wait to submit to him again and again. He could be in charge anytime.

Chapter Four

She cried out as he entered her in one stroke. He set a punishing rhythm, thrusting into her hard and fast. The pleasure was overwhelming, and her mind gave up trying to stay focused. Her senses took over, sharp and unrelenting. She could smell the musk of their arousal and sweat. She could hear their labored breathing and the slap of flesh against flesh. She could feel his cock pistoning in and out of her, rubbing against that spot inside her. The spot that would send her to heaven. She wrapped her legs around him to pull him closer. She was ready for release.

"I bet she is." Brianne laughed. "If she's being ridden that hard and fast, she's probably sore as hell and ready for it to be done."

Lisa giggled. "I love it hard and fast. I mean, if you're going to give it to me, then damn well *give it to me.*"

Sara sipped at her martini. "I like it hard and fast, too, but I know what Brianne means. Sometimes, it's like *are you done?* Jeremy and Cole can last forever some nights. That's twice the sex and twice the thrusts. Especially if they've already made me come a few times…A girl can get sore if she's not careful."

Noelle grinned. "Stop bragging about having two men. But you're right. There's nothing worse than chafed pussy."

Tori tried to hold in her laugh. "Chafed pussy? Geez, Noelle, you have quite a mouth on you."

"I know I do. Don't tell Cam because I get punished for bad language."

Lisa waggled her eyebrows. "You love getting punished. You

don't fool us for a minute."

Noelle sighed. "I do. Luckily, Cam is a real hard-ass about things, so I get punished on a pretty regular basis."

Tori played with her martini glass. "I got my first punishment."

She had their complete and total attention. Brianne leaned forward with a grin. "Well, don't just sit there, woman. Tell us all the dirty details. Was it hot? Is he really strict?"

"He is very strict and exacting. Just as Lisa said he would be. I was punished for hesitating to obey him. He had to repeat himself more than once. I got a spanking." She took a deep breath. "Then, he put me in the corner to think about my behavior and how I might change it."

Every one of her friends was wide-eyed. Lisa took a gulp of her drink. "In the corner? Oh, Tori, that is fucking hot. I'm going to have to find a way to suggest it to Conor without sounding like I'm telling him what to do."

Noelle leaned into the camera. "I've never been put in a corner, but I have had to sit in the barn, naked, and think about what I did wrong. It is very hot. Cam will come in after I've been in there awhile with a Dom look on his face and ask me to explain why I'm being punished. Shit, I love it and hate it all at the same time."

Brianne nodded. "It sounds pretty erotic. But it is a good lesson, Tori. Doms hate to repeat themselves."

Lisa smiled. "Conor has a saying. 'What I want, when I want it, how I want it.' And he sure as fuck doesn't like repeating what he wants. So I take it everything is hunky dory between you two?"

Tori nodded. "We're giving this a try. So far, I really like it. Ian is wonderful, and it is very freeing letting him be in charge. We're not serious or anything, but we are exclusive." She pulled a face. "But he wouldn't, you know, do the deed."

Sara rolled her eyes. "The deed? Are you saying he wouldn't fuck you? How come?"

"He said it was because it was my first night as a submissive.

Don't get me wrong. I'm not unhappy. He's got mad skills, I will say that. I just wish he would have, you know, fucked me."

Noelle took a long drink of her martini. "This conversation is killing me. I'm going to jump Cam's gorgeous body the minute I see him. Fuck, maybe I'll take one of the ATV's out to where he is and we'll have some outdoor fun."

Brianne laughed. "Life would be much easier if our men didn't have to work for a living and could simply be at our beck and call all day."

Sara popped a chocolate into her mouth. "Is Ian still working on the rapist case? I saw him on television last week but haven't heard anything since."

"He is. He's been working tons of hours and seems really distracted by it."

"Are they getting close to catching this guy?" asked Lisa.

Tori shrugged. "I don't know. Ian isn't allowed to tell me too much. They're keeping a lid on some of the details of the case. I only know he's stressed. And worried."

Sara put her hand on Tori's arm. "I'm sure he'll catch him, and soon. I watch those forensic shows now and then, and I'm not sure how anyone gets away with anything anymore. Technology is amazing."

"I'm sure he will. In the meantime, I'll have to make sure he stays happy when he's not working."

Noelle laughed. "It's a dirty job, but somebody has to do it."

Tori lifted her glass with a smirk. "Good work if you can get it."

Lisa pushed the box of chocolates toward Tori. "There's a play party at The Estate in two weeks. Are you and Ian going?"

"The Estate? Ian hasn't said anything."

Brianne tossed her e-reader on the table. "The Estate is a private home owned by a richer-than-God man who likes to give parties. It's been dubbed The Estate because it's huge. It's on the intracoastal. I hope you and Ian go. Nate and I are going, and so are Lisa and

Conor."

"I'll ask Ian about it. Am I ready for a public play party?"

Lisa nodded. "You don't have to do anything, but it would probably give you some exposure to the types of things that go on."

"I am kind of fascinated to see what it would be like. If we go, what should I wear?"

Brianne giggled. "Fetish wear. You can borrow something from me if you don't want to buy anything. But I'd love a reason to go shopping for something new. Just remember, whatever you buy, you won't be wearing for long."

Tori knew her modesty was going to be an issue. Perhaps a play party was the perfect thing to get over it. Sort of like getting thrown into a pool to learn to swim.

"If Ian says we're going, I'd like to go shopping. I want to surprise him."

"Haven't you already?" asked Noelle. "He was ready to go vanilla for you."

"That was never really an option. I don't think he could have done it. This was the only way."

Lisa refilled their glasses. "I think you're very brave, Tori. I admire the way you're going after what you want and being open-minded. People could take a lesson from you."

"Before I give any lessons, let's see how this all plays out. There's a chance this is going to crash and burn."

Sara shook her head. "It doesn't change the fact you've been brave. Not many people would have given this a go, Tori. Ian is a lucky man to have found you."

They were lucky they'd found each other. Now they needed to make this relationship work. She was determined it sure as hell wasn't going to fail because she was a chicken shit. She was going to give this everything she had.

* * * *

Tori pushed through the crowded sports bar and headed to the back. She was meeting Ian here for lunch since his schedule was so busy. Despite the fact they lived next door to one another, they couldn't seem to spend enough time together. They'd spent pretty much every evening together for the last week. One of them would make dinner, they'd watch some television or listen to music, then the clothes would come off.

She now knew why her four book-club friends had big smiles on their faces. Sex was awesome, but sex with Ian was out of this world. He was leading her slowly down the road of submission and she was loving every single second. It was like nothing she'd ever experienced and better than anything she'd read about.

She saw Ian at a corner table, checking his phone. He looked gorgeous today in his blue suit, pressed white shirt, and blue and silver striped tie. A man in a suit, with a body like Ian's, was too sexy for comfort. She could already feel her body responding. It remembered all too well the pleasure his body could bring.

She sidled up to his table with a saucy smile. "You look lonely, handsome. Can I join you?"

His slow grin set her pulse hammering. "I don't know. You're sexy, but I have a girlfriend."

She ran a finger up his arm, tracing his bicep. "I won't tell if you won't."

"You're a naughty young lady. Someone should take you in hand."

She pretended to pout. "I don't mean to be bad. I just can't help it. I need a big, strong man to discipline me."

He flexed his fingers and her pussy flooded with moisture. It was the same movement he made when he was getting ready to spank her.

His eyes narrowed and his grin became wicked. "I'm the man who could do it, but we'd have to set some rules. You'd have to obey me at all times. My word is law."

She nodded, her expression solemn. "Your word is law. Will you punish me now?"

He pulled her down into the chair next to him, laughing. "You're so going to be punished for teasing me like that. Here we are in this public restaurant and there isn't a damn thing I can do about it." He leaned over and gave her a slow kiss. "Hello, little slave," he whispered, his breath warm in her ear.

He pointed toward the iced tea he'd ordered for her. She drank it gratefully, parched from running errands all morning. He sipped his water and quirked an eyebrow.

"Steady, there. You're really thirsty aren't you?"

"I feel like I've been running since the sun came up. It's nice to sit down and have a cool drink."

Ian frowned. "Don't let yourself get dehydrated. Then you wouldn't be able to go with me to The Estate this weekend."

Tori had mentioned the party to Ian last week and he'd said he wasn't sure about them going, so she was surprised to hear him say they were.

"We're going?" She felt a rush of excitement. Lisa and Brianne had bent her ear for the better part of two hours telling her stories about these play parties. She was dying to go but terrified, too. She didn't want to embarrass him with her inexperience.

"We are. You're a star pupil of submission. You've surprised even me by how quickly you've taken to this. We'll go and play a little bit and watch some others. It will give you some exposure to how others play and also give you a chance to ask some questions. It will also give me a chance to punish you for your little role-playing here at the restaurant today. Now I have a hard dick and no relief in sight."

She giggled. "We could go out to my car."

"You're incorrigible, my slave, and you will definitely get punished at the party."

She pouted for real this time. "I have to wait until then?"

"It's two days away. I have to work tonight, and you have your girls' night out tomorrow night. You're all mine after that, though." He dropped his voice. "I'm going to push your boundaries, sweetness."

She fidgeted on her chair. Her whole body was ready and primed and it was a nonstarter. She gave him her sweetest smile. "Since we won't be together for a few days, perhaps you might consider letting me blow off some steam?"

"Steam?"

She nudged his foot with her own, running her toes up his leg. "You know, taking my pleasure into my own hands, so to speak."

He leaned forward, his citrus scent teasing her nostrils. "Aw, sweetheart, it's hard isn't it? The passion, the desire. I feel it, too." He straightened and gave her a stern look. "But absolutely not. No. I want you ready to beg by Friday. Your pleasure comes from me and solely from me. No exceptions."

She sighed. She was ready to beg now. It was going to be a long two days. She wasn't allowed to bring herself any pleasure, and between fantasizing about him and her reading material it was damn difficult.

She stuck out her tongue. "You're a mean Dom."

He laughed easily. "You don't know the half of it, Tori. I warned you, if you remember."

"Hey, Ian. I didn't know you would be here for lunch."

Tori heard a voice, and a large hand landed on Ian's shoulder. Ian turned with a big smile and clapped the other man on the back.

"Tim, I want you to meet my girlfriend, Tori Cordell. Tori, this is my on-again, off-again partner, Detective Tim Mills."

The man was boyishly handsome with dark hair and eyes and an easy smile. She shook hands with him and waved to the chair next to her. "Would you like to join us? We haven't ordered yet."

She didn't really want to share Ian, but it would have been churlish not to offer. The man's lips twisted. "Only for a minute. I'm meeting another guy here, and I'm guessing the last thing you want is a third wheel anyway, am I right?"

Ian got the attention of the waitress and a large water was placed in front of Tim in seconds. Apparently, he and Ian were regulars.

He drank down half the water in one gulp. "So, tell me how you two met and why I can't find women like you."

Tori chuckled. Tim was a charming man. "I'm not sure why you can't find women like me. We're everywhere. Actually, Ian and I are neighbors. He moved in next to me about three and a half months ago."

Ian placed his hand over hers. "The rest is history. Private history."

Tim shook his head. "Yeah, I get it. She's yours and you're not going to tell me any details. Got it. Listen, Ian, are you going to be at the briefing this afternoon? I may need to miss it. I've got a lead I want to run down."

"I'm planning to be there. I can fill you in. You don't want to miss tonight, though. We're going to go through the results from the questionnaires. They're printing up the computer analysis as we speak."

"Is this the rapist case?" she asked. She wasn't sure if Ian would tell her, but she was fascinated by his job. Hers seemed quiet and uneventful in comparison.

Tim grinned, his face animated. "It is. This guy is really smart. We'll get him in the end, though."

"I'm sure you will." Tori thought it was strange Tim was so happy about a serial rapist running loose. Perhaps it was the nature of the job. A sort of gallows humor.

"We're trying to hunt down a person who might be the next victim. Ian got a letter from the rapist with a picture in it of the supposed next victim."

She could feel Ian's body go tense, and white lines appeared around his mouth. He was pissed.

"Tim, we're not supposed to be talking about the case. These are confidential details, man."

Tim shrugged. "She's your girlfriend. I assumed you'd already told her. Pillow talk and all that." He turned to her. "I assume you can keep a secret, then? No one is supposed to know the guy has contacted law enforcement."

She crossed her heart in pledge. "I promise I won't tell a soul. I can absolutely keep this quiet. I only want you both to be safe, that's all."

"There's my friend. I have to go. It was very nice meeting you, Tori. I hope to see you again soon."

Tim left the table as quickly as he'd arrived. She squeezed Ian's hand.

"I swear I won't say anything. You can trust me."

He scraped his hands down his face. "I know I can. Tim's a good cop but almost like a puppy when he's working a case. He gets excited, I guess. God knows who else he's talked to. He's still young. He wants to move up in the department, and I think he gets overeager. You don't make chief of detectives overnight."

"Do you want to be chief of detectives?"

Ian grimaced. "Fuck, no. Too much paperwork and too much talking to the press and the mayor. I'll stick with my job, thank you."

"I thought you liked being in charge." She gave him a teasing smile as he signaled the waitress.

"I like being in charge of you. A bunch of cops, no thanks. Now, let's order lunch. Damn, I wish I was going to be able to see you tonight, Tori. When this case is over, let's plan a little vacation. Maybe a trip to the Keys."

"I love the idea." She raised her iced-tea glass. "To the end of this case."

He raised his glass and clinked hers. "To putting this guy behind bars and heading to the Keys. With you."

"I have just the bikini for the trip."

"I have just the flogger and ball gag."

Heat rushed to every part of her. She fluttered her eyelashes and ran her hand up his hard muscled thigh.

"Yes, Master Ian."

He grabbed her hand and held it firmly. "You just doubled your punishment, little slave. I'd quit while you're not even close to being ahead."

She wasn't scared in the least. It felt like she was getting exactly what she wanted.

* * * *

Tori was fucking late. She'd stayed way too long at the fetish-wear store, and her friends were going to have her ass on a platter. She was supposed to be dressed and ready when they picked her up at eight o'clock. It was seven fifty-six now, and nothing she did was going to slow down time.

She pulled into her garage and breathed a sigh of relief. They weren't waiting for her with impatient-but-amused looks on their faces. They knew she was a stickler for punctuality, and this deviation wasn't going to go unnoticed or unremarked on.

Tori grabbed her shopping bag, her purse, and her phone, juggling her car keys. Maybe she should call them and give them a heads up? Shit, they were already on their way. She needed to get her ass in gear. Calling them would only slow her down.

She slammed the car door shut and headed for the door leading into the house. She could do this. She could get ready in the next three minutes. She looked down at her phone to see if she had a text from Ian. The rapist had struck again last night, the victim he had sent a picture of, and Ian had been working the case all day. When he'd called her this morning, he'd sounded dead on his feet.

She was almost to the door when a gloved hand snaked around her face, covering her mouth. A strong arm wrapped around her torso, twisting her to the garage floor. She struggled against what felt like steel bands, trying to free herself. She kicked at him wildly, hoping to roll him off of her. His hand tore at her blouse and she thought he would win, when she was blinded by lights. A car had pulled into her driveway.

He immediately let her go and started running away, down her street, and into the darkness. Her friends poured out of the car and headed straight for her. Lisa was the first to reach her, a wild look on her face.

"Dear God, Tori! Are you okay? Holy fuck, Brianne, call the cops!"

Brianne fumbled with her phone while Lisa helped her to her feet. She was covered in dust from the garage floor, and her blouse was torn. She would probably have a few bruises where he had pulled her to the floor, but other than that she was unhurt. She sagged against the car, the adrenaline draining from her body.

"I'm okay. Did you see where he went?"

Lisa found her keys on the floor and unlocked the door, wrapping an arm around her to help her inside. "He flew past us so quickly we weren't sure what was going on at first. Thank God we got here when we did. How long had he been here?"

She sat heavily on the couch and wrapped her arms around herself. "Just moments before you got here. He came out of nowhere when I got out of the car. I never saw him coming. He grabbed me from behind."

Lisa filled a glass with some water. "Dressed like the Unibomber with a hoodie covering his face."

Tori reached for the glass, but her hand shook so badly she couldn't hold the glass. Lisa had to wrap her hand around Tori's and help her. Brianne joined them.

"Okay, the cops are on their way and so is Ian."

Tori shook her head. "No, no. I don't want Ian here. He's working an important case. I'm fine. How did you even get his number anyway?"

Brianne held up Tori's phone. "This was on the garage floor. Easy-peasy to find him. Of course he needs to be here, Tori. He's your boyfriend. He wants to be here. He's a cop, after all."

Lisa helped her take another sip of water. "And he's your Dom. Dom's are over-the-top protective. If we didn't call him, I'd be in trouble with my Dom. So get over it. He's on his way."

Tori tried to stand on shaky legs. "I want to change. I need to take a shower."

She wanted the feel of his hands off of her.

Lisa pressed her back on the couch, shaking her head. "I think you should wait for the police in case they want any evidence from your clothes."

Tori shuddered. "They can have these clothes. I'll never wear them again." She took a deep breath. "He was trying to tear my blouse off."

Brianne's eyes were bright with unshed tears. "You're going to be okay. The cops will catch this guy."

"Ian's got his hands full trying to catch the serial rapist. He's trying to clear away work so we can go to The Estate tomorrow night. Oh, shit!"

Lisa reached for the water glass again. "What? Do you need something else to drink? I can pour you a shot of tequila."

She shook her head. "No, can one of you go out and grab my shopping bag out of the garage? I was at the fetish-wear store today buying something to wear to the play party. I don't need Hillsborough County's finest finding my purchases and taking them into evidence."

Brianne nodded. "I'm on it."

Lisa patted her hand. "Just relax. The cavalry will be here soon."

Tori put her head in her hands and closed her eyes, trying to block out the memories of those few frightening moments. She needed to fucking get ahold of herself before Ian showed up. She didn't want him upset by all this. She needed to show him she was strong and capable of handling things.

The house seemed to fill with people all at once. Several police officers were there and they were asking her questions, which she was trying to answer, but her brain didn't want to think about the details. It was only a few minutes later when Conor and Nate walked in the front door.

Brianne looked shocked. "Who's watching the kids?"

Nate put his arm around her. "Our mother. The kids are fine. We left them watching the *Lion King*."

Lisa was hugging Conor. "I'm glad you're here. They're asking Tori questions."

Conor sat down next to her and held her hand, but he addressed the officers. "Ms. Cordell is my client. Has she been offered medical care?"

"I'm fine, Conor. More shaken up than anything. Lisa and Brianne scared him away."

He patted her hand. "My wife can be intimidating."

He was trying to get her to smile, and she tried. "She sure can."

There was a commotion at the door and then Ian was there, kneeling on the floor and holding her hands. He looked shattered.

"Sweetheart, are you okay? Fuck, I was in South Tampa when Brianne called me. It took forever to get here."

Considering he'd made the drive all the way to Westchase in less than thirty minutes, he must have broken a few traffic laws. His voice was urgent, and she could hear the worry and concern. She gave him her best "everything is okay" smile. "You got here pretty fast if you were in South Tampa. I'm fine, Ian. Brianne and Lisa scared the guy away. Is anyone looking for him? He ran down the street and disappeared between the houses."

Ian nodded grimly. "I've got a couple of guys canvassing the neighborhood in case he hung around. He's probably ten miles from here by now. I'd guess he'd have a car parked somewhere down the block."

She took a shaky breath. "You didn't have to come here. I know you have to work."

An expression of anger crossed his face, but he hid it quickly. "You are more important than anything. And this is work. Can you answer our questions? Do you want something to drink or eat?"

Lisa headed for the kitchen. "I'm going to make some coffee. I think we could all use some."

They all drank the coffee and Tori answered their questions, sometimes more than once if she needed to clarify something. Brianne and Lisa also made statements as to what they witnessed. It was exhausting, and Tori knew it wouldn't make a fucking bit of difference. The guy was gone and he would probably never be found. All of this effort by the police was a complete waste of time.

The entire time Ian sat next to her and held her hand. She wasn't ashamed she'd leaned on him during all the questions. He'd been a rock to cling to. When it was all over, he gently asked her to take off her shirt and pants so they could be put in evidence. She was happy to shed them and hopefully never see them again. She stood up to head into the bedroom and Ian followed, pulling on rubber gloves and holding a paper bag.

"Stay still and I'll pull these clothes off of you." He quickly and efficiently stripped her and bagged the clothes, then bagged the gloves. "I'll give these to the officers. Lisa said you wanted a shower. Why don't you go ahead while I get rid of everyone. I think you need some peace and quiet now."

She did need some time to herself. Thanks to Ian, she was much calmer. She was also exhausted. The adrenaline from earlier had drained away, and she was sagging against the doorway of the bathroom. A shower seemed like too much effort. She turned on the faucets and poured some bath salts into the tub. She would take a bath and soak her sore muscles, and if she was lucky, she'd soon be asleep and this terrible day would be over.

Chapter Five

Ian gripped the edge of the dresser, his knuckles turning white. He needed to get control of emotions. His woman needed him to be strong. It was ironic. He saw all sorts of violence and suffering in his job, but when he'd received Brianne's call about Tori...

He'd turned on his flashing lights, run every light, and broken every fucking speed law there was. Every protective instinct in him had welled up, and he'd needed to be there to protect her. His independent little sub was going to fight him and tell him she was fine, but he wouldn't back down. She needed to understand she belonged to him now. He cared for and protected what was his.

He hadn't done a very good job so far. She was in the bathroom, bruised and shaken. He pushed open the door and found her soaking in the bathtub. He knelt next to the bathtub and lifted her hand, twining his fingers with hers. She smiled but didn't open her eyes. He kissed her knuckles, nibbling on her pinky. Finally, she lifted her lids and sighed.

"This night sucked. I was supposed to have fun with the girls. My luck is usually better than this."

His jaw tightened. "I should have been with you instead of working."

She shook her head. "No, you were doing what you needed to do. The people are depending on you to find the rapist."

"My most important job is to protect and care for you, Tori. You come first."

She nodded and sat up, for once uncaring she was nude. "I did come first tonight. You dropped everything and came for me. I'm guessing you drove like a bat out of hell. You can't be with me every minute, and I can't be with you every minute. Don't you think I worry about you? You're a cop."

Ian snorted. "I'm a detective, not a street cop. I'm not in shootouts every day. My job is actually fairly routine. Some might even call it boring. It's not very dangerous."

She rested her chin on their entwined hands. "Do you think he was waiting for me? Do you think he's been watching me?"

That's exactly what he thought, but he wasn't sure Tori was ready to hear it. Still, he'd kept the truth from Tori once. He wasn't going to risk it again. A Dominant doesn't lie to his submissive. Truth was everything.

"Yes, I do think he was waiting for you. He was probably waiting until dark, for an opportunity. It was bad luck that tonight you gave him the opportunity. I wish I had been with you. Where were you coming home from anyway, this late?"

Her cheeks turned a becoming shade of pink, the first sign of color in her face since he'd entered her house tonight. "I was at the fetish-wear store to buy something for the play party tomorrow night. I lost track of time and was running late. I wasn't paying any attention when I got out of the car and was staring at my phone when he came up behind me. I know that's a cardinal sin in self-defense."

"It is. Attackers are waiting for distracted women, looking down at their phones or fumbling with their keys. Always look up, look around, and have a confident air about you. Although, in this case, I'm not sure it would have made any difference."

"He came out of nowhere." Her voice quivered and his heart twisted in his chest. Uncaring of his shirt sleeves, he pulled her into his arms, running a soothing hand up and down her back. She let him comfort her for a long time, drawing strength from him. Eventually, her hands wandered up his chest and she pulled his head down for a kiss. He tried to keep it light and sweet, but her tongue pressed against his lips for entrance. He pulled back with a grimace.

"Tori, honey, the last thing you need is that."

She grabbed at his shirt. "I do need this. I need to feel your hands on me. I need you to take away the memory of his hands. Please, Master."

Her voice was desperate and he couldn't refuse. He understood what she needed now. He would always give her whatever she needed. He lifted her from the tub, her nipples rubbing against his chest, and gently set her feet on the floor. He grabbed a towel to dry her off, his stomach roiling when he saw the bruises on her hips and arms. He wanted to find this guy and slowly tear each of his limbs off of him, then beat him over the head with his own legs. Instead, he lifted her in his arms and carried her to the bed.

"No Master and slave tonight. It's the last thing you need. Just me and you making love, Tori."

He was going to show her how gentle and tender he could be. He was going to chase the bad memories away for this amazing woman.

* * * *

"I need you, Ian."

She held out her arms to him. She needed his warm, rough hands on her body to wipe out the memory of the other set of hands. The hands that had only wanted to hurt her. She wanted the blissful oblivion making love to Ian would provide.

He plucked at the buttons on his shirt and pushed it off his arms, revealing his tan, muscular chest with just a sprinkling of dark blond hair. Her fingers itched to run through it, testing its silky softness. If he were on top, it would tease her nipples, sending shivers of pleasure to her toes.

He popped the button on his trousers and lowered the zipper. It sounded loud in the quiet room, and her nipples and pussy reacted to the blatant sexuality. Her cunt clenched as he pushed his pants and boxers down his legs, revealing every mouthwatering inch he was going to gift her with. She sat up on the bed and reached for his impressive length, running her hands over the velvety flesh. The skin was so soft, but underneath was like steel. He groaned as her fingers traced the veins under the skin.

"God, Tori, it feels so good."

She was fascinated by his cock, a pearly drop of pre-cum leaking from the purple-red mushroom head.

"You're so beautiful. Your body, your cock. I've never thought a cock was beautiful before, but yours is."

She leaned forward and licked at the head, the salty taste of him exploding on her tongue.

"Fuck, fuck. That's your Master's cock, naughty girl. If you make me come, we'll have to wait awhile before we can make love tonight."

She gave him a teasing smile. "So much for no Master and slave tonight."

His features tightened. "Shit. Force of habit. I meant it about it just being us tonight. Forget what I said."

She let her fingers slip down and caress his balls while she swiped at his cock with her tongue. He moaned in response, making her feel desired and powerful. Although she was servicing him, it was clear she was the one in control. Submission didn't seem so scary all of the sudden. It seemed empowering.

"I know I belong to you, Ian. It doesn't bother me or make me scared. I like it. I want it that way."

She did. Ian treasured his possessions, and none more so than her. He would always see to her pleasure and safety. She knew it deep down inside, no doubts.

She sucked him into her mouth until he bumped the back of her throat. She moved her head up and down, flitting her tongue on the sensitive underside. His fingers tightened in her hair and his breathing became labored. She rolled his balls in her fingers and he bit off a filthy word. She almost smiled, but with his cock stretching her jaws wide she instead sucked at the head, running her tongue in the slit. He pulled back, lifting her chin with his finger.

"I'm going to come in your pussy tonight. Lie back and spread your legs. I want a taste first."

His wide shoulders pushed her thighs apart, and she wriggled as his hot breath made contact with her creaming cunt. He ran his hands up her legs, and goose bumps broke out on her skin. Every touch of his hands sent fire licking along her veins, and honey dripping from her pussy. His first touch took her breath away.

She gulped air, and the room seemed fuzzy as his tongue traced her folds before tongue fucking her. She rained cream in his mouth and he licked up every drop and then made more. He scraped his teeth lightly on the sides of her clit, drawing a half scream and half moan from her.

"Please, please make me come."

He didn't make her wait. His mouth closed over her swollen nub and sucked, sending her straight into orbit, her body bowing as waves of pleasure made the room spin and her body shake. She came down to orbit as he rolled on a condom. She beckoned to him.

"Come fuck me, Ian."

* * * *

Her voice was husky and filled with passion. He loved watching her come apart as she climaxed. Her eyes would darken and then close tightly, her lips parted and panting. Her skin flushed a rosy color, and her body would tighten and then tremble, her toes curling. It was a beautiful and humbling sight. Tori trusted him enough to let herself go, even after her attack. He would never betray that trust. It was sacred to him.

He moved on top of her, her nipples teasing his chest, her warm, wet pussy pressed against his belly, and captured her lips with his.

Their tongues rubbed and tangled, her taste exquisite and arousing. He kissed a trail down the soft, fragrant skin of her neck to her full, round breasts. He would love to restrain her seeking hands and clamp her rosy nipples, but tonight wasn't the night. There would be time enough for that another evening. Many other evenings. Tonight was about treating Tori like a goddess.

He ran his tongue around her nipples, and her back arched and her fingernails dug into his biceps. He blew on the wet peaks and watched them tighten further. Her eyes were closed, her teeth sunk into her bottom lip. He pulled a taut bud into his mouth and sucked, scraping his teeth gently. She reacted by grabbing his head and pulling him closer. He obliged and sucked at her nipple until she was twisting and moaning underneath him. He moved to the other nipple to make sure it received equal treatment. She was begging for his cock before he was done.

"Fuck me, Ian. Fuck me hard."

He moved up her body and shook his head. "I'll fuck you, sweetheart, but not hard. I'm going to fuck you slow and sweet tonight. We're going to meld together as if we're one person."

He lined up his cock and pressed forward slowly, her muscles giving way with her gasp of pleasure. Her pussy hugged him tightly, so hot and wet. It was heaven. Pure fucking nirvana. He wanted to be deep inside her as far as he possibly could, inside her skin. He groaned when he was in to the hilt, his cock bumping her cervix. She moaned and wrapped her legs around his waist, her hands clenching his shoulders.

He stayed there and looked deep into her green eyes. He wanted to see into her soul, and he wanted to bare his own. He couldn't remember the last time he'd made himself this vulnerable to a woman, but tonight it seemed very right. He pulled out almost all the way and then slowly pushed back in, sparks of pleasure running from his cock straight to his balls and lower back. With each stroke, he could feel the pressure building in his lower body.

Tori's nail raked his back and he gritted his teeth, trying to hold back. He could feel the ripples in her cunt. She was close. He reached down between them and rubbed circles around her swollen clit. She screamed his name, her pussy gripping his cock like a vise. Ecstasy ran through his veins like water, and he gave in, muttering an oath under his breath. The pleasure burst from him and seemed to shake his very core. He shot his seed into the condom, his cock jerking, his face buried in her neck. Both their bodies were covered with a sheen of sweat, and he bit into the flesh where her neck met her shoulder, marking her as his woman.

He lay on top of her, catching his breath and feeling the waves of aftershock from her cunt. He pushed her tangled hair back from her face and caught her lower lip with his mouth, nibbling and licking.

"You're insatiable." Her voice was soft and hushed in the afterglow.

"For you? Yes. But I think I need to take care of this condom before we even contemplate continuing this." He pulled regretfully from her body and headed into the en suite bathroom. He paused to look into the mirror, expecting to somehow look different. He looked the same, but he didn't feel the same. Tori had taken residence in his heart. When he'd received Brianne's call tonight his world had tilted on its axis. Only seeing Tori, holding her in his arms, made it right.

He took a deep breath and let himself smile. He was falling in love. He didn't fight the feeling but let it burrow into his heart. For the first time in years, he felt complete. He hurried back to the bedroom, determined to tell her how he felt.

He stopped dead in his tracks and grinned. His beautiful, sexy woman was lying in bed, dead asleep and snoring.

He chuckled. "I guess I wore you out, sweetheart."

As much as he wanted to join her in bed, he dropped a kiss on her forehead and headed out to the kitchen to scrounge a bite to eat and make some phone calls. Finding the son of a bitch who attacked Tori was high on his to-do list. He punched some buttons on his phone and grabbed some leftover chicken from the fridge.

"Tim? I need your help. Listen, I need you to do some checking for me. We've got a case to solve."

Chapter Six

"Lisa and Brianne, eat your hearts out."

Tori slipped into the four-inch black-and-silver high heels and twirled around, checking her reflection in the mirror. She loved this outfit. What there was of it. She'd brought home three different outfits from the fetish-wear store, but this was by far her favorite. It was also by far the most revealing.

The sleeveless minidress was constructed of loosely woven silver chain mail, surprisingly comfortable. When she'd picked it off the rack, she'd expected it to poke and stick, but the links were smooth and rounded, feeling cool against her skin. Underneath the open mesh, she wore a black demi-cup bra and black thong panties. The bra further scandalized by covering only the lower half of her nipples so the chain mail would rub them, keeping them hard with her every movement.

She left her wavy hair loose around her shoulders and wore slightly more makeup than usual. Lisa and Brianne had encouraged her to use a dramatic hand when applying her eye and lip color. Her green eyes were now lined with dark kohl and three coats of waterproof mascara. Her lips were shiny and bright red with matching nails and toes.

"Tori, are you coming, sweetheart? Have you changed your mind? We don't have to go if you don't want to."

Ian's knock on her bedroom door dragged her away from the mirror. He'd argued with her this morning about going to the party, insisting she'd want a quiet evening at home nursing the bruises she'd received. She'd quickly let him know he wasn't getting out of taking her. In truth, she was dying to go to the party and she wasn't letting last night's incident stop her. Just because some jerk knocked her on her ass didn't mean she was going to sit there. She'd pulled herself up and was standing on her own two feet again.

With a little bit of tender loving care from her Dom last night.

She walked into the living room on shaky legs, hoping he approved of her outfit. Lisa had warned her that Doms could be maddeningly picky about the dress of their subs. Add in how exacting Ian was, and this could spell disaster.

He was pacing, looking dark and dashing in his black suit, black shirt, and black tie. She grabbed her tiny handbag from the table and whirled around.

"I haven't changed my mind. I just took too long to get ready. Are we going now?"

She gulped as his eyes darkened and took in every detail of her appearance. He walked around her, inspecting her from every angle. She stood there not knowing what to say or do. Finally, she started to speak.

"Ian—"

"Hush, slave. I am inspecting my property." He held up a hand and she went silent. "Before we go out or start a scene, I will always inspect your body and make sure you are groomed to my specifications."

Tori knew what grooming he referred to. When he had told her they were going to the party, he had also told her his slaves were to have a bare pussy. She'd shaved carefully today but decided it might be easier to be waxed going forward. Much more painful but much easier.

He leaned down and ran his hand up her bare leg from her ankle to her inner thigh, sending tingles straight to her cunt. He nodded before his fingers went straight to her pussy, pulling on her already wet crotch and running his fingers on the bare skin.

"Good, slave. You followed my directions. From now on, I expect your legs and cunt to be smooth. Raise your arms."

She raised her arms and he inspected to make sure she had shaved there, also. It was a little embarrassing, but once again, it wasn't a deal breaker. She was logical enough to realize this was to put her in a submissive frame of mind. He probably couldn't care less if her underarms were shaved. This was simply to help her get in the right head space for the coming evening.

"Lower your arms."

He ran his hands all over her exposed skin and she shivered with pleasure from his rough fingertips. It looked like his lips twitched, but the moment was gone and he was looking at her with a stern expression.

"I'm very pleased. Your skin is smooth, soft, and fragrant. Your pussy is already wet with arousal, and your nipples are hard. Exactly as I want you. We need to go over the rules for tonight. I want you on your best behavior."

He pointed to the floor and she looked down at her shoes. He didn't like her shoes? These were expensive Jimmy Choos.

"When I point to the floor, it means kneel at my feet."

Ooooohhhhh. She wanted to roll her eyes but fought the urge.

"I think it will help you listen to the rules if you are in a subservient position."

She knelt on the rug and tried to get comfortable, wondering how many damn rules there were. She didn't want to embarrass him tonight, but she didn't want so many rules she couldn't remember them, either.

He placed his hand on top of her head. "When we get to The Estate, you do not have permission to speak, unless I give you permission or ask you a direct question. If someone addresses you, look to me, and I may or may not give you that permission. Also, try to avoid looking Doms directly in the eye. It is considered rude. You don't have to look down at the floor, but boldly meeting their gaze is a no-no. Also, when I sit, you sit at my feet. When I am standing, you stand slightly behind me and to the right. Any questions?"

"No, Master."

His finger circled her neck. "I would like you to wear a collar to the party to signify my ownership." She heard his chuckle. "I don't want anyone thinking you're an available sub."

She looked up at him. "I don't have a collar. I could get one of my necklaces. I think I have a few short ones."

He smiled. "No, pet. I have one for you if you consent to wear it. It's only a play collar for the party, not a permanent collar that indicates something far more serious."

She felt honey drip from her pussy. She shouldn't like being on her knees and called "pet," but she did. She fidgeted and nodded her agreement. She was shocked at how much she wanted the collar around her neck, even if it was only a play collar.

He pulled a chain from his jacket pocket and held it up, before placing it around her neck. A heart-shaped lock snapped into place. He lifted her chin.

"My God, you look beautiful with the collar on. The tag says 'Master Ian's pet.' You will be my pet tonight. I'm going to give you an introduction to scening you won't forget. Now stand please."

She stood on trembling legs. The mere presence of a collar around her neck made her feel incredibly submissive to Ian. She wanted to kiss his black, polished shoes and beg to serve him. Part of her fought those feelings, but she knew they were from doubt and fear. She didn't want either of those emotions tonight. She pushed them back ruthlessly. She wanted the pleasure and ecstasy her Master could bring. And he could only bring it if she trusted him.

"Are you ready to go, Tori?"

"Yes, Master. I'm ready."

She really, truly was.

* * * *

"It's huge."

Tori looked at the imposing structure of The Estate. "Estate" was an excellent description. It was sprawling with an enormous main house and a few smaller buildings. It was nestled overlooking the intracoastal, and knowing Tampa Bay real estate as she did, was worth tens of millions. She'd never cared to be this wealthy, but she had to admit it was beautiful. She could smell the salt air from the water and feel the Gulf breeze.

"It is huge. Montrose made his money in oil and real estate, I believe. He's hard-core into the lifestyle."

"He's a Dom?"

Ian chuckled. "No. He's a sub. Powerful people often want to give up control. They don't want to be in charge every second of the day. He has a girlfriend, who is not interested in dominating him, and a Domme for times like this."

She certainly understood not wanting to be in charge all the time.

"He submits to someone who's not his girlfriend? How can he do that if he doesn't have any feelings for her?"

"I didn't say he didn't have feelings for her. I said she wasn't his girlfriend. Hold out your wrists for me, beautiful slave."

She stood next to his car and held out her wrists, fairly certain of what came next. He quickly and efficiently wrapped wrist cuffs around them, buckling them in place. She lifted them to have a closer look. The cuffs were a soft, padded leather with Ian's initials in silver lettering. He was marking her as his property in more place than one.

"What do you think?"

She twisted her wrists so she could see them from every angle and tugged on them to see if they'd budge. They didn't. "They're comfortable and soft. I guess I expected handcuffs from a cop."

His laugh was soft and warm like the night. "Handcuffs are decorative, but in a scene can leave marks unless they're padded. You'll be able to wear these all night and be comfortable." He reached and clipped the cuffs together so her hands were restrained.

"You'll still be able to move your arms, but you'll get a taste of cuffs. One more thing."

He pulled a long leather cord from his right jacket pocket and clipped it to her collar. "A leash. It will keep you from getting separated from me at the party and also show you are not available. Okay, let's go. Remember the rules."

He wrapped the leash around his hand a few times so she was following him closely, and they headed for the entrance. She wasn't too sure how she felt about being put on a leash but let it go for now. She'd liked everything else so far. Logically, what he said made sense about not getting separated. If it became an issue, she'd talk to him about it.

He led her into the large foyer where he stopped and handed identification to one of three large men who must have been doormen. They obviously knew Ian, as he laughed and joked with them. They didn't even glance her way, not acknowledging her existence. Their lack of attention made her feel better about her skimpy attire.

He led her deeper into the party and she tried to take everything in at once. Lots of people mingling, talking and enjoying a drink. Several subs knelt next to their Dominants, and many were on leashes such as herself. It was easy to tell the Doms from the subs. The Doms wore clothes and the subs were nude or almost nude. Several of the Doms were dressed as Ian was, in black, while some were dressed in black leather. She could feel eyes on her body as they walked through the crowd of people. She didn't know if it was because she was new or because she was with Ian. It couldn't be because she was practically naked. There were too many naked bodies in this room for hers to be much of a novelty.

He led her into another room, much darker, and the music was louder. The scent of leather, sweat, and sex filled the air, and she realized he had brought her into a play room. In one corner a Dom was flogging a sub covered in tattoos on a St. Andrew's cross. Her bright red hair was pulled up in a ponytail, and her body was shiny with sweat. Her back was arched, and by the expression on her face, she was enjoying every minute of her whipping.

Across the way, a male sub was bent over a bench and getting beaten with a paddle on his bright red buttocks. The Dom was grunting with the power of every blow, and even this far away she could hear the sub begging and pleading for mercy. She looked at Ian uncertainly. He followed her gaze.

"I can assure you he's fine. They play this scene all the time. He likes to be paddled and he likes to beg. It's part of their kink."

"He's not going to be able to sit for a week."

Ian nodded. "He'll like that. It will remind him every day of the fun they had here tonight. I'll introduce you later if you like, and you can see for yourself he's okay."

She squirmed as her cream dripped down her thighs. Every scene in the room was erotic. Just to her left a sub was on her knees sucking her Dom's cock. Another sub was over his Domme's lap getting a spanking. To her right, a pretty sub was bent over, restrained in stocks, getting fucked from behind. Tori's pussy burned with need. She was already fantasizing herself in those stocks with Ian behind her.

"Do you like that? Are you picturing us there together?" Ian's voice was close, his warm breath tickling her ear.

She swallowed and nodded, not taking her eyes off the couple. He began using a crop on the woman's thighs as he pounded in and out of her. Her screams of pleasure and pain mixed with the heavy bass of the music. Tori's own heart sped up as the woman climaxed, her face rapturous.

Ian tugged on her leash and led her into the next room. This one was just as dark but quieter, with classical music playing. The same toys were set up and people were playing, but this room seemed more restful. He led her to a corner and unclipped her leash, dropping it into the large gym bag he had carried from the car.

"We'll play here." He pointed to the floor, and this time she knew what to do. She sank to her knees and bowed her head slightly. He placed his hand on top of her head. "Do you wish to serve me, slave? Do you wish to submit to your Master?"

Arousal was sizzling in her veins. Watching the others play hadn't scared her. Far from it, it had turned her on. She couldn't wait to experience what Ian had in store for her tonight.

"Yes, Master. I wish to serve you."

"We'll take it easy tonight, but you will learn to serve me, slave. Kiss my feet and we will get started."

Cream gushed from her pussy as she leaned forward and placed her lips on one shoe and then the other, the leather cold underneath her mouth. He reached down to help her stand and unclipped her wrists.

He pointed to a table with a padded leather cover. "That's a bondage table. I think we'll start there tonight. But first, let's take off this very sexy but in-the-way outfit."

His eyes were dark blue with passion, his expression stern. He wouldn't permit her modesty tonight. Luckily, the lights were low and everyone seemed busy elsewhere. She pulled the chain-mail dress over her head and placed it in his waiting hands. Her bra and thong followed until she was standing in a room full of people butt naked. She didn't turn to see if anyone was checking her out.

"Good girl. Keep your eyes on me at all times. Don't worry what others are doing while we're in our scene."

She'd watched others. She knew people would watch them but pushed it out of her mind. She'd never had much of an exhibitionist bent before, but if people got off on watching her with Ian she was okay with it. At least she was okay in this time and place. These were strangers. Strangers who were just as naked as she was. She could also see there were all shapes and sizes of women here. It was some comfort.

While she sure as hell wouldn't want anyone watching them in the privacy of their home, The Estate seemed to strip the veneer from a person, leaving their inhibitions at the door and inviting their inner beasts to come out and play.

"On the table, slave. Lie down."

He helped her onto the table, pressing her torso down and clipping her wrists above her head. He wrapped a soft strap just above her knee and repeated the process on her other leg so her knees were pulled up and wide, exposing her creaming pussy to his and anyone else's view who might walk by. He pressed a finger inside her cunt, drawing a moan from her.

"You're dripping wet, my little slave. Remember, you do not have permission to come until I tell you."

She stared up at the ceiling, completely black but for what looked like hundreds of small spotlights casting shadows around the room and playing peekaboo with bare, writhing bodies. She took a deep, centering breath harking back to her yoga days. She heard him rummage in his bag and then he was holding up something in front of her eyes.

"I'll give you the choice tonight. Blindfold. Yes or no?"

She shook her head, wanting to see his expressions, the look in his eyes. He nodded and placed it on a cart next to the table. He bent down to his bag once again, and this time showed her a flogger, its long strands hanging down. It looked quite innocent but in the wrong hands was probably a painful weapon.

"It's velvet. I think you'll like this. What is your safeword?"

"Red."

"What do you say if you need me to slow down or take a break?"

"Yellow."

"Good girl. Let's see how you like the flogger."

The strands ran up the inside of her thighs and down her legs, almost tickling in their sensation. She felt her lids get heavy as the strands trailed all over her body, caressing and sensitizing her skin. The first strike was soft on her outer thigh. Her other thigh was next, working up and down her legs and inner thighs. A few of the strands landed on her drenched pussy, and she moaned at the contact. She arched her back, offering up her breasts for his attention. His eyes glowed when he caught her action, and he moved the strikes up her torso, gently thudding on her belly and then finally her breasts and nipples, sending streaks of heat to her cunt.

He started striking her harder, the impact sending heat skittering through her body and cream dripping from her needy pussy. Her nipples were tight buds, desperately waiting for the sting of the strands.

"What color are you at, slave?"

His voice penetrated her erotic haze. She licked her lips. Words were an unwelcome interruption. "Green, Master."

"Good girl." His hand brushed her hair back from her face and caressed her jaw.

The strikes built in intensity, the strands stinging and sending heat to every corner of her body and making her cunt clench with need. He flogged the tender skin of her inner thighs, the strands stinging her swollen pussy and clit. She moaned and panted, needing something but not quite sure how to reach it. He paused, his hand on her belly.

"What color are you at, slave?"

"Green, Master, but close to yellow."

"Good girl. Very good girl. We'll take a break then." His hand stroked the skin of her belly in a soothing motion. He trailed his fingers down into her pussy and teased her clit, making her gasp and groan.

"Did you like your first flogging, slave?"

"Yes, Master," she panted. She was close to coming without permission. He stilled his fingers to give her a chance to catch her breath and get her arousal under control. She heard the flogger fall to the floor and the rustle of the gym bag. He held up the next tool of torture. It looked like a miniature whip, toddler sized.

"It's a very small whip. It concentrates on a small area. Are we green, slave?"

She was back in control and nodded. "Green, Master."

He leaned over her torso and flicked his wrist, bringing the tiny whip down on a tender nipple. The sting and pain were immediate, and she yelped in surprise. It was much more direct than the distributed strands of the flogger. He waited, his expression remote, as the pain turned to heat in her nipple and traveled straight down to her slit. She felt drops of her honey slide from her cunt down to the edge of the table.

Another flick of the wrist, and her other nipple was the victim. The stripe of heat made her cry out and shudder with a mini-orgasm. Ian leaned close to her ear.

"Sweet slave, what color are we at?"

She gulped in air. "Green, Master."

He didn't immediately respond, his intense gaze raking her from head to toe, but he finally nodded. "You have permission to come, slave."

He positioned himself between her legs, and she knew where the whip was going to land next. The first strike was aimed at the inside if her thigh, low and close to her cunt. He didn't pause but peppered her inner thighs and low buttocks with the tiny stripes, making her wait for the inevitable.

Her body was strung taut, every muscle tense, her body bathed in sweat, as she waited. She couldn't stop the words tumbling from her lips, her need was too great.

"Please, Master! Please!"

The whip came down on her clit. Her body shattered into a million pieces, her arousal soaring. The lights seemed to twirl and spin as pleasure suffused her entire body. She'd never felt anything like it. She was almost down to earth when she heard his zipper and the crinkle of a condom.

She sighed in relief as he thrust in to the hilt, stretching her pussy and rubbing her G-spot.

"Yes, Master. Fuck me."

* * * *

He was going to ride his sweet slave to oblivion. Her pussy was tight and so wet he slid in easily. He grabbed her thighs and began to ride her fast and hard, completely opposite of how he fucked her the night before. There was a time for slow and gentle and a time for hard, hot, and sweaty. It was clearly time for the latter.

She was tugging at the restraints, moaning and panting, as he slammed into her cunt over and over, grunting with each thrust. His vision was going blurry, and his body felt like it was on fire. He leaned over and caught a nipple in his mouth, worrying it with his teeth. She screamed his name as she went over the cliff again. The ripples of her cunt dragged his climax from him. It burst from his balls and out his cock, jetting his seed into the condom and leaving his legs wobbly. He took in gulps of air as he locked his knees to stay standing and rode the waves of pleasure until he was drained. He pulled away regretfully and quickly disposed of the condom in the discreetly placed receptacle.

His slave needed aftercare. He unclipped her wrists and removed the bindings from her thighs. He massaged her body, getting the circulation moving before slipping an arm underneath her back and lifting her to a sitting position. He grabbed a bottle of water from his bag and placed it at her lips, letting her drink until she pushed it away. A blanket was next, and he lifted her into his arms and carried her to a couch not far away, cuddling her to his chest and loving the feel of her body next to his.

He snuggled with her for a long time, letting her drift in her special world, stroking her hair and whispering soft words. He barely noticed when a submissive brought his bag and her clothes over with a bow. Tori's lashes fluttered, and she was looking straight into his eyes. He felt his heart squeeze in his chest at the emotion he saw reflected there. She was as overcome as he was. He traced her lips with his fingers.

"I'm so proud of you, sweetheart. Your submission is such a gift tonight."

Her submission had been more genuine and more heartfelt than any he'd ever experienced. This woman truly wanted to please him. She also truly cared about him as a person, not just a Dom she could get multiple orgasms from. He was humbled and at the same time exultant. She was the submissive he had waited to find. No more Devil Dom snarking at immature, self-involved subs. He'd found a true lady with a woman's heart.

She captured his hand with her own. "Did I do okay?" Her smile was breathtaking.

He let his stern Dom facade crack. "No, you did better. You did awesome. You were amazing."

She chewed her lower lip. "Can we do it again?"

He grinned. "Absolutely. But let's take a breather. Maybe you might want to walk around and see some of the other rooms? Maybe we can get some fresh air, too."

She nodded and pushed the blanket away, then realized she was naked. She tried to pull it back, but he just laughed and tossed it away.

"The horse is out of the barn and the gate firmly closed behind it, little slave. I will let you put your bra and panties back on if you kiss me very sweetly."

She didn't hesitate, her lips locking with his and their tongues tangling. He pulled away and grabbed her clothes from on top of his bag.

"You earned it. Bra and panties. Nothing else."

She pulled a face and stuck out her tongue but did as she was told, wriggling into her clothes. He folded up the chain-mail dress carefully and stowed it in his bag. It was very unique, and he didn't want anything to happen to it. Tori looked spectacular in it. He'd want her to wear it again and again.

"You stuck out your tongue and made a face at your Dom, slave.

Not a good idea. You'll be punished for that."

Her mouth fell open in shock. Apparently, she thought teasing a strict, mean Dom whose nickname was Devil was a good idea.

He would show her the consequences for not showing the proper respect. He gave her an evil smile and reached for the cups of her bra.

* * * *

"I'm sorry, Master."

Ian's hands were warm, his thumbs brushing her nipples when he pulled the cups of her bra down and tucked them under her breasts.

"Thank you for apologizing, slave. Your punishment stands, however. I think you need a reminder of your place."

He rummaged in the leather bag, and this time he held his hand out, palm up and open.

Nipple clamps.

She recognized them from some internet searching she'd done after reading her first BDSM book. They were the screw type with little rings hanging from them. Her nipples tightened instinctively and her stomach clenched. He was going to put those on her. She remembered all the times she'd fantasized as she had looked through those websites, all the toys and restraints. One of her fantasies was coming true. Tonight.

"Play with your nipples. Get them hard and tight for me, slave. You will participate in your punishment."

She was beginning to realize why he was called the Devil Dom. It was one thing to be punished. It was a whole other thing to be party to her own punishment.

"Yes, Master."

Luckily, her nipples were already taut with arousal. She rolled and tweaked them between her fingers anyway, her face hot. She'd never touched herself in front of a man before.

"Harder, slave, and keep your eyes on me."

She swallowed hard and locked her gaze with his. His eyes were a molten blue, on fire with desire. She pulled harder at her nipples, pinching them until she almost winced. He nodded his approval.

"Good girl. Hands behind your head."

She placed her hands behind her head, her breasts lifted in offering. He placed the cold metal around her nipple and tightened the screw relentlessly. She was helpless to stop the squeezing of her already-sensitive nubs. She kept her eyes on his, biting her lip as the clamps bit into her flesh. Finally, she could take no more and winced. He backed the tension down immediately, but the pressure remained. It felt strange to have constant squeezing of her nipples. The pain sent pleasure to her cunt and clit, and she shifted on her feet. Ian frowned.

"Stay still and take your punishment."

He repeated the process on the other side, once again backing the pressure down when she visibly couldn't take the pain. He reached back into the bag and pulled out a long piece of leather, holding it up. It was shaped like the letter *y* with a loop on one end and tiny hooks on the smaller ends.

"This is a leash. These will hook onto the rings of the clamps so I can lead you around by your nipples. Once again you will participate in your punishment. Bring your hands down and attach the leash to your clamps."

She knew better than to hesitate, but her hands were shaking as she hooked first one side of the leash to the ring on the clamps. She snuck a peek at Ian. He was waiting patiently, the stern Dom expression on his face, his arms crossed over his chest. When she finished the other side, he nodded.

"Good girl. You'll find your participation in punishments will be frequent. I think it is important a sub is not passive in her punishments but fully active in the implementation. The result is you'll think twice about disobeying me. Also, it indicates to me you acknowledge your bad behavior and are accepting your punishment. Now, slave, do you need to use your safeword?"

She shook her head. She was already thinking twice about disobeying him. Suddenly, disobeying just to see what he might do seemed like a terrible idea and not fun at all. He clipped her hands together behind her back and picked up the looped end of the leather leash, wrapping it around his wrist.

"We'll walk around and see some of the scenes. You have permission to speak only to me. I want to encourage you to ask questions and let me know what you feel as we look at things. Come, slave."

Chapter Seven

Tori's eyes were darting everywhere. His beautiful sub was taking everything in and getting aroused. He could see her chest rise and fall with her ever-quickening breathing and the pulse beating at the base of her throat. She was incredible, and tonight she belonged to him.

The scene he'd done with her was still reverberating in his mind and body. Her submission had been sweet, her responses addictive. He could get used to playing with her.

She'd also taken her punishment with a maturity he'd come to expect. Requesting she assist in her punishment was an important step in their relationship. It was her formal acknowledgment of his dominance and authority in meting out those punishments. So far, she hadn't come close to using her safeword, but he intended to push her boundaries even more tonight.

She froze in front of a scene with a blonde sub strapped to a St. Andrew's Cross and a tall Dom dripping candle wax down her breasts. Wax play had been of particular interest to Tori. She was mesmerized now. Ian even gave the leash a playful tug to get her attention, but she only licked her lips at the sensation and kept watching the couple.

"It's beautiful, isn't it? Look how she arches her back, inviting the wax to drip down her body. She submits to his will completely."

Tori nodded, her gaze never straying from the scene. The woman's expression was dreamy, and her Dom was whispering in her ear before each drip of the candle. It was an erotic picture. Ian felt his cock pressing against the zipper of his pants, visualizing himself and Tori in the same position. She would be beautiful painted in wax.

"Does...does it hurt?" Her voice was a whisper, as if speaking too loudly would break the couple's concentration. The couple, however, was in their own world, completely unaware of the audience they had attracted. The loud music would have kept them from hearing their voices, in any case.

"It can. Using the right kind of wax is essential. Beeswax melts at a much higher temperature, so it's not a good choice for wax play. Actually, cheap candles are a good choice. I find the plain white utility candles are the best."

Tori watched as the Dom let the wax drip lower, down the sub's belly, a few drops disappearing into her pussy. The sub jerked against the restraints and hissed as each trail of wax covered the sensitive flesh of her mound and thighs. The Dom whispered something in her ear and moved the candle so the wax would drip onto her clit.

"He probably just gave her permission to come. As soon as the wax hits her clit she's going to go off like a rocket. Watch, Tori."

He pulled her back against the bulge in his pants so her bare bottom could rub against it, making his balls ache and his teeth grind. As soon as this scene was over, he was going to find a quiet corner and fuck Tori's brains out.

As if in slow motion, the Dom tipped the candle and the wax dripped down her mound, toward her clit. He felt his slave tense in his arms as she, too, waited. She had put herself firmly in the sub's place. Ian wouldn't be surprised if Tori came when the sub did, so strongly she seemed to identify with the scene. Ian decided to give her a little help and slid his hand in her thong, rubbing her swollen clit and tugging on the leash attached to her nipples just as the wax hit the sub's clit.

The sub screamed her ecstasy, pulling at the restraints and calling to her Master. Tori exploded at the same time, crying out in surprise as her body shook in his arms and her honey covered his fingers. The Dom kept the scene going by allowing a few more drops to trail into the sub's pussy. Ian played with Tori's clit until she was boneless, her knees turned to jelly. He unclipped her hands trapped between them and swung her up in his arms, carrying her over to a long sofa. He signaled to a waitress.

"You okay, pretty slave?"

Her eyes were unfocused but she nodded. "Yes. I'm okay. God, it was so intense. I can't believe I came from just watching them."

Ian chuckled. "Watching them and my fingers. I love that you were able to get so wrapped up in their play. A good scene is intense. Obviously, wax play turns you on."

She nodded again, still slightly dazed. He took the two sodas from the waitress and handed one to Tori.

"Drink. The sugar and caffeine will help you."

Tori drank deeply. "I could use a real drink after that."

"No way, slave. BDSM and liquor don't mix. If we were here only watching, yes. When we're playing, absolutely not. No impaired judgment allowed on the Dom or the sub's part."

"That makes sense. I'm glad you keep me safe."

A warm glow took root in his chest. "I will always keep you safe. Hey, Conor, Nate. It's good to see both of you tonight."

Ian grabbed a large cushion and tossed it on the floor next to him, pointing to it. It was a test for his pretty submissive. It was one thing to submit to him in private or around people she didn't know. Would she sit at his feet in front of people who knew her? Conor and Lisa Hart and Nate and Brianne Hart had walked up and joined them. These were some of Tori's best friends.

He waited for the mutiny, preparing himself to deal with a recalcitrant sub. He almost sighed in relief when she lowered herself to the cushion after only a moment's hesitation.

This might go well after all.

* * * *

Tori arranged herself comfortably on the pillow. It was a little embarrassing to be sitting at Ian's feet, but one look at Brianne and Lisa told her Nate and Conor wouldn't think anything of it. Brianne was dressed in only stockings, garters, and high heels. Her wrists were clipped to her collar, but she gave Tori an encouraging smile. Lisa, on the other hand, couldn't smile. Her mouth was stretched wide with what looked like a huge ball gag. Her wrists were clipped in front of her with a chain leading down to manacles on her ankles. She was being led by a leash attached to a wide, black leather collar. Lisa's head was bowed, her eyes trained on the floor.

Nate took a seat, tossing a cushion on the floor for Brianne. He stroked her hair and whispered something in her ear, making her smile. It was easy to see the love between the two of them. Nate worshiped Brianne. Conor also sat, tugging on Lisa's leash. She knelt between his legs, facing him, but her head down. Conor grimaced as he patted her head gently.

"Please excuse my slave's anti-social behavior. She is on punishment right now." He looked down at his wife with an indulgent smile. "My slave needs to learn to curb her tongue. Until she does, she'll find herself gagged and chastised. Ian, may I address your slave?"

Ian's hand caressed her hair. "Yes, you may. Tori, you may speak to Conor."

"Tori, how are you feeling after what happened last night? This question is to both of you, I guess. Have they found the guy who did this?"

It was hard to take her eyes off of Lisa, who was being uncharacteristically quiet and meek, but she dragged her gaze away to answer Conor.

"It's very sweet of you to ask. I feel okay. Just a few bumps and bruises, that's it. I'm just so grateful Lisa and Brianne showed up when they did."

Brianne smiled but didn't say anything. Nate pushed a long strand of auburn hair back from her face and nodded. Brianne leaned down and kissed his foot before turning to Tori.

"I think I speak for Lisa, too, when I say we're so happy we showed up and scared that asshole off. I hope they catch this guy."

Tori opened her mouth to answer, then closed it quickly, realizing Ian had only given her permission to speak to Conor. She looked up at him and his smile was warm and approving. "You may speak to all four, well, three of your friends," he said, giving Lisa a rueful glance. She was still kneeling between Conor's legs.

"They haven't found him yet. Ian's had several cops canvassing the neighborhood, but no one but you two really even saw him. He was behind me and I never got a look at him."

Brianne's lips tightened. "I'd like ten minutes with this guy. When I think about seeing you on the garage floor, fighting him off, shit, I get so mad."

Nate lifted Brianne's chin to look into his eyes. "I gave you permission to speak, not permission to curse. Watch your language, slave."

Brianne fluttered her eyelashes, and Tori could swear she saw Nate actually melt.

"What will you do if I don't, Master?"

Nate leaned in close, grinning. "Paddle your bottom."

Brianne's eyes lit up. "Well, damn, Master. Bring it on."

Nate pulled Brianne to her feet. "Sorry, but we're going to play. Say, goodnight, Brianne."

"Goodnight," Brianne called over her shoulder as Nate led her away. They were both smiling, and Tori had a feeling Brianne was going to have a wonderful night.

Conor unbuckled the ball gag and pulled it out, wiping Lisa's chin. "This can't stay in any longer, but I want you to continue to be quiet, slave. You're still not in the clear."

"Yes, Master." Lisa never looked up, continuing to kneel with her head bowed. Tori was amazed at Lisa's self-discipline. She'd never seen Lisa that still or that quiet in all the years she'd known her.

Conor leaned back on the couch. "You're working the serial rapist case, right? Do you think there's any connection between Tori's attack and that case?"

Tori stiffened in shock. It had never occurred to her the man who'd attacked her could be *the guy.* Apparently, it had occurred to Ian, as he didn't take long to answer.

"We don't think so, but we're not taking any chances, of course. Tori's clothes were sent to the lab to see if we can get any evidence or DNA off of them. If they can, it will be compared to samples from the other assaults." Ian was massaging her shoulders, kneading the tight muscles. He must be able to feel the tension in her body. She looked up at him and he shook his head. He didn't want her to speak.

"Conor, I'm going to give Tori more of a tour of The Estate. Good luck with your slave tonight."

Ian helped her to her feet, holding firmly on the leash. He gave it the slightest of tugs, and arousal shot from her nipples straight to her clit. She tried to hide her shiver, but Conor grinned.

"My slave simply needs a good dose of discipline. I've reserved the stocks tonight."

Lisa never moved, but Tori shuddered. The stocks looked positively medieval.

Ian led her deeper into The Estate and then out a set of large French doors onto an enormous screened-in patio. The warm breeze caressed Tori's bare flesh and teased her already-hard nipples. Ian waved his arm to the corner.

"It was getting hot in there. I thought we'd play out here. It's unseasonably warm tonight but cool enough we won't get overheated."

She was already more relaxed, but she needed to ask him a question.

"Permission to speak, Master?"

"You have permission to speak to me, Tori. Although I think I know what you're going to ask. You want to know about the serial rapist, don't you?"

She nodded, relieved he was open to discussing it. "Yes. You really don't think they're one and the same? Honestly, until Conor mentioned it, I never thought about them being the same person."

"I know. I could tell by the way your body stiffened up and got tense. No, I don't think they're the same person. The MO for The Boyfriend is different. He attacks people in parking lots and garages, secluded areas. He's never gone after anyone in their own home before. Generally, a perp doesn't change their spots when things are working for him."

"The Boyfriend? Is that what the cops call him?"

Ian's face closed down. She knew he wasn't going to say anymore.

"It's a nickname. Please forget I mentioned it. I really can't talk about this. I'm sorry."

"I understand. I really do. I'm just glad you think it's not the same guy. If it was, I would be afraid he would come after me again."

He reached behind her and unclipped her wrists, massaging her shoulders.

"Maybe you should come stay with me for a little while. Just until we catch this guy, of course."

She arched an eyebrow. "Of course. I guess I would be spending a lot of time naked should I take you up on this offer."

He nodded. "Probably. I told you I like a naked sub. It's still warm this time of year in Florida. Clothes would just get in the way."

She rolled her eyes. "So logical. I'll think about it."

Ian's eyes narrowed. Shit, she was in trouble. She played their conversation back in her head to find where it had gone wrong, but couldn't see it.

"Rolling your eyes at your Dom is a bad idea, little slave. You need a paddling for your blatant show of disrespect. In addition to the punishment you already earned that day at lunch. Teasing me is never a good idea. Let's get you over to the spanking bench."

She followed his gaze to the leather-covered contraption in the corner. He dropped her leash so she could walk around it, examining it from all angles. It was easy to see her ass was going to be in the air and vulnerable.

He beckoned to her. "First, we need to remove your leash. Kneel before me and ask me humbly to take off your leash."

She swallowed and did as he commanded. She knew from her reading this was going to hurt like a bitch, but her body was already humming with arousal at the promise of the erotic pain.

"I didn't put them on all that tightly, but they've been on awhile and this is really going to hurt, slave. Ask me for it."

She licked her lips, her honey dripping down her thighs. "Master, please remove my leash. I'm ready for the pain."

He indicated she should stand, and reached for the first clamp. "I doubt you're ready for the pain, slave. I'll help you this time."

Before she knew what was happening he had pulled her to her feet, unscrewed one clamp, tossing it aside, and replacing it with his mouth. He sucked as the blood rushed back to the sore nubs. She grabbed his head as her knees buckled. The sensation was overwhelming, pleasure and pain all mixed up. She had barely caught her breath when he repeated his actions on the other side. A moan slipped from her lips and a gush of cream leaked from her pussy.

He held her up until her legs could hold her. "Good girl. You were very brave. I'm proud of you."

"Thank you, Master." Her voice was shaky and she tried to steady herself, taking a deep breath. There wasn't much time to catch her breath before he was leading her to the bench. He helped her kneel on the padded base of the bench. Her ankles and knees were efficiently strapped down, and his hand pressed on the middle of her back, pressing her onto the cool leather. She breathed deeply, her nostrils teased with the smell of Ian, leather, and lilacs from The Estate grounds.

Her arms were stretched out wide, as if she was playing airplane, and clipped into place. He stroked her spine softly, his rough fingertips sending arrows of pleasure directly to her cunt and clit.

"Do you need to use your safeword, Tori? It's okay if you do. There's no shame in using it."

It was comforting to know she could use it at any time. She trusted all play would immediately stop, but she didn't want to stop it now. She craved this spanking. She needed it.

"No, Master. I'm green."

"Very well. Let's get you into position."

He reached under the platform where her legs were cuffed and flipped a switch, sending her thighs wide apart. A warm breeze from the trees ran over her overheated pussy and teased her clit. She wriggled on the platform, inviting his hand on her ass cheek. He reached under the bench supporting her torso and angled it downward, pushing her ass even higher in the air.

"Perfect. Now you're ready for your spanking."

She heard him open his bag, and then he was holding a wood and leather paddle in front of her.

"Kiss it, slave."

She pressed her lips to the leather nervously. He'd always spanked her with his hand. Tonight was going to be different. This must be what he meant by pushing her boundaries. He rubbed her bottom, getting blood to the surface. This was his usual procedure, so it wasn't a shock when his fingers delved into her drenched pussy and played with her clit.

"If you want to come, you have to take your punishment. Are you ready, slave?"

"Yes, Master." She was nervous but excited.

"Ask me humbly to punish you."

This was harder than the actual spanking. He made her request her own punishment. She was logical enough to know why he was doing it. It was a signal she wanted the spanking. She didn't have to enjoy asking for it, however. She took a deep breath.

"Please, Master, punish me for my transgressions."

"Do you deserve to be punished, slave?"

Out of the corner of her eye, she could see they had attracted a small crowd. His voice was laced with steel and his hand was firm on the small of her back. Lisa and Brianne had made it clear. Her actions reflected on her Dominant. She wouldn't let him down. They'd agreed to the rules, and she'd broken them.

"Yes, Master. I deserve it." Her voice was clear and strong. She heard a murmur of approval from the onlookers.

"Then you shall be punished. A paddling for your disrespect. No set count. We'll go until your ass is nicely hot and your attitude is adjusted."

He made her wait. He paced back and forth, taking her in at every angle. Finally, he stepped to her left, rubbing her ass cheeks again. She flexed her hands in the restraints, impatient to get the punishment underway.

When the first strike came, it took her breath away. The paddle landed with a resounding thud on her bottom, and it quickly turned to heat. She tried to arch her back, begging for more and letting him know how much she wanted it. Each stroke of the paddle ratcheted up the heat on her ass cheeks until they felt like they were on fire. She was pulling against the restraints restlessly, needing respite for a moment.

"Where are we, slave?"

Tori panted. "Green, Master. Very close to yellow."

His hand stroked her hair. He bent low to whisper in her ear, his breath warm and comforting. "Will you be displaying any more disrespect, slave?"

"No, Master. I will respect you."

"Good girl. Time for your reward. You took your punishment well. I always reward good behavior. I think you need to come."

Tori's ass, nipples, cunt, and clit burned and tingled. She needed to come more than she needed to breathe.

"Please, Master."

"I love it when you beg. It's time for you to scream."

* * * *

Ian dropped the paddle into the leather bag and knelt between her spread thighs. They were shiny with her honey and her clit swollen out of its hood. It left him in no doubt regarding how much she'd enjoyed her paddling.

He ran his tongue along her folds and heard her indrawn breath. She was already on the edge, and playing with her would be cruel, no matter how much he loved her sweet cream in his mouth and the musky smell of her arousal. He let his tongue wander to the swollen nub and circled it over and over, feeling her body tremble on the brink.

"Come for me, Tori."

He closed his mouth around her clit and sucked gently. Her scream reverberated through the outdoors, echoing off the canopy of trees. Honey gushed from her pussy and her body tensed, her fingers and toes curled. He played with her cunt as she came down, licking and nipping at her inner thighs. He stood and massaged her thighs and back, her skin soft and smooth.

"Where are we, slave?"

For a moment, he didn't think she was going to answer. "Green, Master."

"Good girl. One more toy and then I'm going to fuck you hard. Do you want that?"

Her voice was breathless but excited. "Yes, Master. Please fuck me hard."

He pulled the small plug from his bag and dripped lube over it, soaking it completely. If she'd never had anything there, he would need to have patience as she took her first plug. He patted her bright red bottom.

"I'm going to insert a beginner butt plug, Tori. I want you to relax and push out against it. Can you do that for me?"

She was trying to strain her neck to see it but was restrained too well.

"Yes, Master."

He walked around and held the plug so she could see it.

"You wanted to see it? It's the smallest they make, with a flared end so it will stay in place. You're going to wear it until we get home tonight."

He didn't imagine her eyes growing darker with arousal. She was starting to climb to orgasm again and he'd barely touched her. She was an incredibly passionate woman, and he was grateful he was the recipient of those emotions.

She nodded, apparently satisfied. He returned to his position behind her and spread her cheeks, pressing the plug against her back hole. He dripped more lube down her crack and pressed gently but insistently. She was panting and tensing her legs.

"Relax for me. You're too tense. Push out."

He heard her take a breath, and then the tight ring of muscles gave way and the plug slid into place. He pressed a kiss on each rosy ass cheek.

"Excellent. How does it feel?"

"Full. I feel full."

He chuckled. When he eventually fucked her there, she was going to think this plug was a walk in the park. She didn't know what full really meant.

"It's a good starter plug. We'll work up to taking my cock. Are you in any pain, slave?"

She was starting to move restlessly in the restraints.

"No, Master. I just need you to fuck me. The plug is making me tingle, and I need your cock."

She liked having something in her ass. She was going to love it when he took her there.

He grabbed a condom and suited up, lining his cock up with her dripping cunt.

"Fucking starts now."

He thrust to the hilt in one stroke.

"Yes!" Tori screamed her approval. He didn't bother to start slow. He fucked her hard and fast, riding her rough, her hot, wet pussy hugging him tightly and sending his libido through the roof. He could fuck her forever, stay in her snug cunt all night, feeling it milk his cock. He felt the pressure building in his balls and knew he wouldn't be able to hold on much longer.

His head fell back and he stared at the ceiling, trying to think mundane, boring thoughts to hold off his climax. He'd managed to hold back the tide when she tightened her pussy on his dick rhythmically and he cursed, feeling his balls draw up tight.

He reached around and pinched her clit, sending her over the edge. She screamed his name, her cunt clamping down on his cock. The ripples from her orgasm did him in. His climax ripped from his balls and shot hot and fast into the condom. His entire body froze, the intensity of pleasure more than he'd ever experienced. He loved fucking this woman.

When it was over, their bodies were bathed in sweat. The smell of sex hung in the night air. Ian pulled from her body regretfully. He felt complete when he was inside her, giving them pleasure. He quickly disposed of the condom and removed her restraints. She was limp and sated with a dreamy smile on her face.

Hell, I've probably got the same look on mine.

He wrapped her in a blanket and carried her over to the nearest couch, cuddling her close and pressing chaste kisses to her forehead and cheek, her skin petal soft under his lips. She needed to be treated like something precious and rare. Her gift of submission must be acknowledged and rewarded.

He lifted her chin so he could see in her gorgeous green eyes.

"Thank you, Tori. Your submission is such a treasure."

Her smile was blinding.

"You're welcome. I never thought it could be like this."

"It's never been like this before. At least for me. I'm going to take you home and give you a bubble bath, feed you, cuddle you, maybe give you a back rub. How does that sound?"

She giggled and his heart squeezed in his chest. "Like I won the lottery. How did I get so lucky?"

He pressed his lips to hers, her taste sweet and warm. "I'm the lucky one. Let's go home."

Chapter Eight

Ian shoved his cell phone in his pocket and headed for the precinct exit. It had been a long, frustrating day of getting nowhere on The Boyfriend. He was taking Tori to dinner tonight with some of her book-club friends and their husbands. The last week, having her at his house, had been wonderful.

She challenged his ideas and took him out of his comfort zone regarding politics, religion, family, books, and even movies. Sometimes, she challenged him not because she disagreed but to yank his chain and make him explain why he believed what he did. She was logical, brilliant, and she could argue with him for hours about any subject. He adored a woman who could tie him up in intellectual knots.

As long as he got to tie her up in real ones.

They'd worked out a treaty of sorts. All day they were equals, but when the dinner dishes were done, Tori would strip to her bare skin and be submissive. It was the perfect compromise. One which brought them both a great deal of pleasure.

He grinned as he remembered two nights ago when her sons had called her from college. She'd scrambled to cover herself with a throw from the couch as if they could see her through the phone. He'd behaved while she talked to her boys but then tied her to his four-poster bed and ravished her afterward.

"Taggert, we need you in my office."

Ian blew out a breath in frustration. The chief of detectives was asking for his presence, and saying no was not an option. He turned and followed Chief Detective Harris Martin, a twenty-five-year veteran and a pretty good guy. He wouldn't have pulled Ian into his office unless it was important.

Ian took a seat and wasn't surprised to see Tim Mills there, too.

"This must be about The Boyfriend."

Harris nodded and placed a piece of paper between them. "This is a copy. The forensics guys have the original. You got another letter. Seems The Boyfriend wants to keep in contact with you. Another picture, too." Harris set a snapshot of a pretty young woman with blonde hair between them. "We're running facial recognition on the woman, but you know as well as I do, we're looking for a needle in a haystack."

The contents of the letter were brief.

I have another woman in my sights. Are you impressed with my genius? When I'm done I'll be famous, my picture on television and in newspapers. More roses will be gifted. If you're looking for the answer, you're in the right neighborhood. I want her the most.

"What's so special about this woman? Why does he want her the most?" Ian stared at the picture and shook his head in frustration. He'd never seen her before. She didn't even look vaguely familiar.

Harris Martin stood and started pacing his office. "Good questions. Another question is why has he glommed on to you as his pen pal? Yes, you were on television at one of the crime scenes, but the chief of police has been on television every night talking about this case. Why does he identify with you? Does he look like you? Are you the same age? Maybe he wanted to be a cop when he was a kid."

Ian leaned forward, his elbows on his knees, studying the letter. "I don't know why it's me. I wish it weren't, honestly. Shit, do you think I like some whack job identifying with me?"

Tim waved his hand. "This guy isn't crazy. He's crazy like a fox. He's got us chasing our tails. Doesn't seem like the work of someone who's nuts."

Ian shrugged. "Personally, I think he's a sociopath with narcissistic tendencies, but think what you like. My job is to put him behind bars. He's made this personal for me."

Harris nodded. "You're not alone in this, Taggert. The entire department is with you. But I want you on this case one hundred percent. Hand over your small cases to Stevens. I want your focus on this." Harris pointed to the letter. "He says we're in the right neighborhood. That tells me he's someone we've already questioned. It also sounds like he wants to be caught. He wants to be famous. We need to revisit our suspects. Get them in here and interrogate them. Double-check their alibis."

Ian stroked his chin. His gut was telling him something wasn't right. "Chief, we've talked to a couple of dozen men, and not one fit the profile. Plus, they didn't know any of the details we're keeping secret. When he says neighborhood, he could mean he lives or works near the latest victim. The key here is the victim. He wants her the most. We need to know why."

Harris nodded. "You have a point. Mills, you go back through the suspects we've already questioned and recheck their alibis. Taggert, you work on the girl. Take some cops and canvass the university. She looks young. Check bars, restaurants. Find her and find out why she's so important. We need to find this guy before he strikes again. The press and the mayor are breathing down my neck."

They started to leave, but Harris halted them for a moment. "And for the love of fuck, don't talk to the press. Keep your face off of the television. Keep a fucking low profile, okay? Now get out of here."

Ian headed straight for the exit. After dinner tonight, he would work on a plan to find this woman before she was assaulted. He was more determined than ever to put this guy behind bars. Since The Boyfriend had singled him out for communication, it put the onus firmly on his shoulders to stop him.

It was his responsibility now.

* * * *

"You look stressed." Tori grabbed Ian's hand as they entered the dimly lit restaurant. Despite running late from work, he'd insisted he wanted to keep their dinner date with her friends.

He took a deep breath and straightened his shoulders. "I am stressed. But I promise your friends will never know. This case isn't getting any better. It's only getting worse. I received another letter and picture today."

"I'm not worried about what my friends think. If you need a night to yourself, I can have one of them drive me home after dinner. I don't want you to sit here and wish you were someplace else." She placed her hand on his solid chest. "I want to hear about the letter and picture."

Ian shrugged. "Not much to tell. We don't know who she is, and his letter was as cryptic as the last one. My job is to figure out how to find her before he hurts her." He brought her knuckles to his lips. "And why the hell would I want to be anywhere but with you? I see your friends are already here. Let's eat. I'm starving."

Tori was hungry, too, and they joined Lisa, Conor, Brianne, and Nate at a large table in the corner. Sara was in Illinois with her men, and of course, Noelle was in Montana.

Ian shook Conor and Nate's hands. "Sorry we're late. It's my fault. I got stuck at work. I hope you haven't been waiting long."

Lisa laughed. "We just got here, too. Conor and Nate love their jobs so much they never want to leave them."

Conor wrapped an arm around his wife's shoulders and laughed. "My beautiful wife exaggerates. I love my job, but I love my family more. Although the way the kids were acting before we left, perhaps I should have stayed at work longer."

Lisa frowned. "They act up when you work too much."

Conor looked like he was going to argue when Brianne broke in. "What are you going to order, Tori? I can't decide between the salmon and the lasagna."

Tori was relieved. There seemed to be some tension between Lisa and Conor lately. "I'm getting the chicken parmesan. It's my favorite, and I pretty much order it every time."

Brianne studied the menu as the waiter took their drink order. Tori ordered a Cosmo. She needed to relax tonight even if Ian wasn't going to. She'd been hard at work on her latest book all day.

"I'll get that, too. What about you, sweetheart?" Brianne placed her hand on Nate's with a smile.

Both Nate and Conor Hart were handsome men. Conor was a year older and had a rakish air, while Nate was all-American handsome. Nate's warm blue eyes were soft as he gazed at his wife. "Chicken marsala, pet. I order it every time we come here."

"Don't you want to try something new?" Brianne teased.

Nate whispered something in her ear, turning her cheeks a bright red. Tori grinned at her friend's bashful expression. Brianne couldn't be all that modest, in reality. After all, Tori had seen her practically naked only a week ago.

Nate sipped at his wine. "Ian, Conor says you're working that rapist case. Are you making any progress?"

Ian's body stiffened next to hers. She really wanted him to kick back and relax tonight, but it didn't look like it was in the cards.

"I am working the case, but I'm really not supposed to discuss it. I'm sorry. I will say that our forensic team is working hard and we have moved as many resources to this case as we can. It's only a matter of time before he slips up and we get him."

Nate nodded. "I understand. Conor works on cases he can't discuss, and I have patients I can't talk about. Don't worry about it."

Ian smiled. "I appreciate your understanding. How about I change the subject? I want to hear how you ladies all ended up in a book club and friends."

Conor laughed and shook his head. "I love hearing this story. It brings back some good memories of when we were younger."

Lisa feigned shock. "We're not old. We're still young. I love this story, too. It's not very exciting, but it does bring back memories. I met Tori in college, actually. We had sociology and psychology together our sophomore year."

Tori rolled her eyes. "What Lisa doesn't mention is that I was already married with the twins when we met. She was the original college party girl, and I was trying to go to college and take care of a family. We couldn't have been more different."

Lisa grinned. "True. I kept seeing Tori come to class and fall asleep. It was a large lecture hall and she sat at the back. Snoozing. One day class ended and she didn't wake up. I waited until everyone left and woke her up myself."

"She scared the hell out of me," Tori confessed. "I thought for a moment it was the professor."

"So I invited her for coffee. She discovered caffeine, and presto! She stayed awake during classes from then on. Not that she needed to. What I didn't realize when I woke her up is she came to get some quiet time from her kids and get some sleep. She didn't need to come to class. She's a genius. I don't think she ever cracked a book in college. She's the only reason I passed calculus."

Ian laughed. "You'd never had coffee until then?"

"No. My parents wouldn't let me have any, and then my obstetrician wouldn't let me have any. If I hadn't met Lisa, I might have gone through life never discovering the joys of a caffeine buzz in the morning."

"I can't believe you'd never had soda either," Brianne said. "Your childhood was very restrictive."

"It was. Perhaps if my parents hadn't been so protective, I wouldn't have been so damn naive and got knocked up at seventeen. Not that I regret my boys. I don't. I love them to death. But it might have been nice to have been young and wild."

Brianne waggled her eyebrows. "You can be wild now."

Ian pulled Tori close and she breathed in his masculine scent.

"She can be wild with me."

Everyone laughed, and Conor poured more wine from the carafe, refilling their glasses. "Lisa and Tori were inseparable. Luckily, we all got along really well. We stayed friends through weddings, kids, well, everything."

Tori knew what Conor didn't say but was thinking. They had been together through all those milestones plus Carl's long illness and death. Lisa and Conor had been shoulders she had leaned on many times. They were true friends.

Nate passed the bread basket. "Brianne and her first husband, Rick the Dick, moved into Lisa's neighborhood and became friends. That's how she met Tori, too. Soon they'd started talking about books they liked. Noelle was added when she designed a bracelet for Lisa. Sara was added when she moved into the neighborhood. Mostly, I think the book club is an excuse to drink, eat chocolate, and talk about men and sex."

Brianne giggled. "Our secret is out."

Ian quirked an eyebrow. "I don't think it was much of a secret. Damn!"

Ian's phone was vibrating in his pocket. He frowned and looked at the screen before giving her an apologetic look.

"Can you get a ride home with Lisa or Brianne? I need to head into the station. We may have a lead on the guy who attacked you."

Tori's heart leaped in her chest. "I'll go with you."

He shook his head and stood up. "You stay here. I'm not dragging you down to the station to sit while I interrogate a suspect."

"But—"

"No, Tori. I'll call you if we need you." His voice was deep and firm, sending shivers down her spine and straight to her pussy. She loved it when he used his Dom voice. One quick glance at Lisa and Brianne told her they were well aware of her state.

He leaned over and kissed her hard, beating a hasty retreat. She watched until he was out of sight. Lisa and Brianne had wide grins.

"Good thing you're not getting serious with Ian. He's only completely and totally perfect for you," Lisa teased.

Tori picked up her wine glass, her smile dreamy. "I may have been a little too quick to judge when I said that."

Brianne's eyes twinkled. "You've fallen for the Devil Dom? Good for you, Tori."

It was good for her. Ian had given her something no man ever had. He had given her what she needed.

* * * *

He stroked her silky hair, cut short and spiky, tipped in blue. She was different than his usual long-legged, long-haired, sophisticated business women he usually bedded. This woman had barely noticed him and he'd been following her around with his tongue out, begging for a date.

They'd had their date and now they were half-naked on her couch, making out like two horny teenagers. His cock ached, pressing against his zipper, wanting to be free. Her nipples were hard underneath his palms, and he could smell her arousal in the air.

She wanted him as much as he wanted her.

He slipped his hand down the smooth skin of her belly and under the waistband of her jeans, seeking her heat. She moaned when his fingers found her wet and swollen, but she pushed him away, fumbling with the fastening of her bra. He was shocked. She was turned-on and ready.

"Baby, what's wrong? I want you so much."

She shook her head. "I should have told you."

Dread started building in his stomach. "Told me what?"

"It's just, I really liked you. I wanted to go out with you."

"I wanted to go out with you, too. What do you need to tell me?"

Her eyes were bright with unshed tears. Jesus, was she really a guy or something? Married? Dying? What the fuck?

Her lips trembled. "I'm a virgin. I promised my father on his deathbed I would stay a virgin until my wedding night."

The words were out before he could stop them, but then, the cock was a powerful persuader.

"Then we'll get married."

"Oh my God, this book is a hoot." Noelle laughed. She had tears leaking from her eyes. The book had been sexy and funny so far, and the women loved it.

Tori was holding her side. "I think this may be the best book we've read in months. It's hilarious. This guy is a total horn dog, but he may have met his match in this one."

Lisa refilled their martini glasses. "I knew a guy just like this in college. Remember Neubaum? He couldn't keep it in his pants. He'd fuck anything that moved. Then he met that sweet little librarian. She led him around by his dick for the next two semesters until she dumped him for that rock band. That's what's going to happen to this guy."

Tori nodded. "I do remember him. She had him completely pussy whipped. I think he asked permission to pee. I'm surprised she didn't put a collar and leash on him."

Brianne laughed. "Speaking of collars…Things looked pretty cozy with you and Ian last night. Are things getting serious? Have you talked about a permanent collar yet?"

"I want to know what he found out. Lisa said he got called away from dinner last night because they may have a lead on your attacker," Noelle interjected.

Tori looked at Lisa, who smiled. "I had insomnia last night, so I called Noelle. She's two time zones over, you know."

"You should have called her this morning after I called you and Brianne with the news."

"Which is?" Noelle pressed.

Tori shrugged. "No news. False alarm. They caught some guy

wearing a dark hoodie trying to steal some poor woman's purse. After they questioned him, they found out he was at work the night I was assaulted. Several witnesses were able to verify it."

Noelle rolled her eyes. "Nice to know criminals can hold down a job these days. Still, it must have been disappointing."

"I wasn't getting my hopes up. Ian warned me the speed of justice is slow."

"You're more patient than I am." Noelle smiled. "I'd be climbing the walls." She sipped at her drink. "Listen, I have something I want to talk to you all about. I've met some really nice women here in Montana. They're a lot of fun."

Lisa arched an eyebrow. "Are you breaking up with us? Or breaking up with Cam?"

Noelle rolled her eyes. "Neither. What I wanted to bring up is whether we're open to adding more women to our book club. These ladies are nice, fun, and they read the same kind of smut we do. I think they would make good members."

It had been the four of them until they added Sara, who was currently in Illinois. They'd never discussed expanding the group before, but then it had never come up.

Tori shrugged. "I'm not against it. I assume they would Skype also, or you could have some meetings on your own up there."

Brianne was getting excited, moving restlessly in her chair. "I could start a private group on Facebook so we could all communicate. Sara could add people from Illinois if she wanted to. Fuck, we could have chapters all over the country. This could be huge!"

Lisa laughed and shook her head. "All from our little meetings, talking about erotic books."

"Don't forget the chocolate and booze." Tori laughed.

"I could never forget that. It's the best part." Lisa popped a truffle in her mouth with a grin.

"Is that a yes?" Noelle asked. She was smiling, too. Everyone seemed happy about the idea of growing their numbers.

They all looked at each other and nodded. Lisa raised her glass for a toast. "It's a go. To the Martinis and Chocolate Book Club. Long may it live, long may it reign. And what the hell, long may it inspire us to do sexy things with our men."

They all clinked glasses, Noelle clinking hers against the camera.

Brianne bit into a dark chocolate. "This gets us back to my original question about the men in our lives. Are you and Ian serious?"

Tori pondered how to answer. She'd started this relationship with no intention of making a long-term commitment. Yes, she'd wanted someone in her life, but she wasn't looking for external symbols such as a ring, or in this case, a collar.

"We haven't discussed a permanent collar. I don't know what you mean by serious, actually. Are we exclusive? Yes. Am I falling for him? God, yes. Who wouldn't? Am I freaked out about falling for him? Yeah, a little. I didn't intend to. I really just wanted to meet a man I could have some fun with."

Noelle barked with laughter. "That's how it started for all of us. So what happens now?"

"We haven't discussed the future. Not in concrete terms." She played with the stem of her glass. "We've talked about vacationing together. We talk about plans in the immediate future. He even made a remark about liking me living in his house and how wonderful it was. But has he asked me to live with him, straight out? Nope."

"Do you want to live with him? Wear his collar? Commit to him?" Lisa asked, her eyes narrowed.

A great question.

Tori answered it carefully, her words measured. "Sometimes. It's wonderful having someone in my life I can depend on. Ian's an old-fashioned man in many ways, and I can really count on him to do what he says he'll do and to be there for me. On the other hand, I like my independence. I was a wife and a mother for so long. It was nice to only have to think about me."

Noelle snorted. "Those days are already gone, aren't they? You're already thinking about his happiness. I bet you made his favorite thing for dinner last night."

Tori shook her head. "Actually, Ian made my favorite thing for dinner last night—a thick juicy steak. He's a good cook. Almost as good as I am."

Lisa chuckled. "Okay, the night before, then. It's clear to anyone who sees the two of you, you're ass over tea kettle for each other. I bet you give him back rubs after a hard day at the police station. You'll be wearing his collar before you know it."

Tori ran her finger around the base of her neck. She'd liked the feel of the collar at the play party. Ian's collar wouldn't be a burden, she was sure. It would be a symbol of their commitment, and yes, their love. They hadn't used the *L* word yet, but she was pretty sure it was where they were headed. Soon.

"I'm going to let things progress at their own pace. I'm not pushing it, and I'm not holding anything back. If we make a lifelong commitment, that's great. If we don't, that's fine, too."

She suddenly felt bereft at the thought they might not be together. It was an uncomfortable feeling, the fear. She had to acknowledge her feelings were deeper than she had ever planned.

Lisa pushed the box of chocolates toward Tori. "Our Tori is always so calm and logical. Love has little to do with logic, however. You're in love. So is Ian. Watching you two dance around it is going to be interesting. Give in now and save yourself some time."

Brianne laughed. "She's right. Ian looks at you like you're a goddess. Give in and be happy. Nothing is going to go wrong. This is the right guy."

* * * *

"He was the wrong guy." Tim Mills shrugged. "We'll get the right guy next time."

Ian knew the truth of the words, but he was still frustrated. After hours of interrogation, the guy was guilty of no more than trying to grab a handbag. He would probably be out of jail before lunch today. Ian was still no closer to finding the man who attacked Tori and no closer to putting The Boyfriend behind bars. He was having a lousy day.

"I know. We just need a break in the case. Something we can go on."

"We got it. We've got your break, Taggert."

Harris, the chief of detectives was grinning ear to ear. He must have overheard Ian's remark.

"We have a break? Since when?"

Harris waved a piece of paper. "Since now. One of the patrol officers found your girl. She's a waitress in a bar near here, some place called O'Shea's. Some of the cops hang out there after their shifts. Fuck, of all places to find her. She was in our own neighborhood."

Ian shook his head. He knew of O'Shea's but hadn't been there in over six months. He loved his fellow officers, but he didn't like to spend all his free time with his coworkers. If he grabbed a beer with another cop, it was usually a quick one and at the sports bar about three miles from the station.

"That's amazing. It's great, though. Did the officer talk to her?"

Harris threw the piece of paper down on Ian's desk. "Not yet. That's for you and Tim to do. There's authorization to run a twenty-four-hour surveillance on her. We need to catch this guy when he goes after her. Get her to agree, then get the detail together. We're going to get him this time."

Tim hopped to his feet with a grin. "Damn right we're going to get him. Let's go talk to her, man. I can feel something big is going to happen."

Ian let himself smile for the first time regarding this case. It did seem things were looking up.

"Let's go catch a bad guy. I'm tired of this asshole always being one step ahead of us. This time, we're a step ahead of him."

With renewed determination, Ian grabbed his car keys and headed to O'Shea's. They needed to talk to this girl and start surveillance before anything happened to her.

Tim was right behind him as they entered the elevator. A thought occurred to Ian.

"O'Shea's is a cop's bar, right? Do you think this guy could be in law enforcement?"

Chapter Nine

Tori stretched her arms over her head and yawned, hearing a few pops in her back. She'd been sitting at her laptop for the last three hours straight, working on her a new series of chapter books for slightly older children. It was fun, but she was exhausted. She'd been writing on and off since six this morning when Ian went to work.

She heard the front door and whirled around in her chair, her heart beating faster as she caught a glimpse of his gorgeous face and body. He was an incredibly handsome man, and he was all hers.

At least for now. She wouldn't think about it today and wonder whether his feelings were as strong as hers. According to her friends, he was as mushy about her as she was about him.

His sexy grin sent shivers through her body and her pussy and nipples responded quickly. They remembered what his hands and mouth could do, and they wanted more. Much more.

He pulled her out of the chair and laid a hot kiss on her lips, which she returned with heartfelt fervor.

"How's my girl? It looks like you were hard at work."

She giggled, snuggling close, loving the scent of his body. "I did work hard today. Writing is a dirty business."

Ian waggled his eyebrows. "Especially the books you read. Maybe you should try writing an erotic romance sometime. It would certainly be a change from your usual day's work."

Tori felt her cheeks grow hot. She'd thought about it a time or two but hadn't worked up the courage. "I don't know whether I have enough imagination."

"I think you do, little slave."

His voice dropped an octave and the timbre made her catch her breath. He'd used his Dom voice, and her cunt immediately started to cream. He'd trained her well.

She ran her hands up his chest, feeling the muscles bunch under her fingers. "You're in a good mood, Master."

He grinned. "Ask me about my day."

She would indulge this momentary whimsy. He'd drop back into Dom mode soon.

"Okay. How was your day?"

"It was fantastic. We found the girl in the latest photo and put a detail on her twenty-four-seven. We're going to catch this guy. Soon."

He looked like a weight had been lifted from his shoulders. He looked more carefree than she'd seen him in months. She hugged him, feeling his heartbeat under her cheek.

"That's wonderful. I knew you'd get him."

"We don't have him yet. But we will. I know just how we should celebrate."

She looked in the kitchen, guilt making her wince. "I hope you're talking about going out to eat. I was so busy writing I didn't start dinner yet. I know it was my turn. I'm sorry."

He leaned down and began to lick and nip at the curve of her neck, making her giggle and sending arousal flying through her veins.

"I wasn't even thinking about food. We can order a pizza. Later. I have plans for my slave."

She moaned as his tongue traced a path to her ear, biting the lobe. "Right now?" She was breathless with desire.

"Now." He was firmly back in Dom mode, his voice commanding and dark. "In the bedroom, strip, kneel in position, and wait for me, my slave. Go."

Tori fled to the bedroom, stripping off her shorts and T-shirt on the way, her body already trembling with anticipation. She truly belonged to him, body and soul.

Her clothes landed in the hamper, and she sunk to her knees on the soft rug next to the bed, her nude body reflected in the floor-to-ceiling mirror on the closet door. It was no accident he had selected this spot for her submission. He was determined she would overcome her modesty. She had come a long way. It no longer bothered her to be nude with him.

She rested her bottom on her heels, spread her knees wide, and placed her hands behind her head, thrusting her breasts out. This was his favorite position for her. Her mind was already going to a submissive place inside her. She felt calmer and more serene, knowing she was going to be able to hand over control to him. She had no worries in this room. He shouldered them all.

She closed her eyes and let the silence wash over her. He left her waiting for several reasons, but one was to get her head in the right place. He didn't want it cluttered with unpaid bills, errands, and long to-do lists. He wanted her centered and focused on herself and her own needs and desires.

She heard him walk in the room but kept her eyes down, enjoying the game of wondering what he would do. He moved around the room, turning off lights and lighting candles, before pulling his naughty leather bag of torture tricks from the closet. She concentrated on her breathing as her arousal heightened. She couldn't wait for what he had planned.

His shoes came into her line of sight and placed his hand on her head.

"Tori, do you wish to submit your body and mind to me? Do you wish me to take you under my command and control?"

She licked her lips. "Yes, Master. Please allow me to serve you."

"Very well, slave. Show me your submission."

She leaned forward, keeping her knees spread and her hands behind her head, and pressed a kiss to each of his well-shined shoes before resting her forehead on the floor, awaiting his first command.

"Your submission is a gift, slave. I will protect and care for you. Lift your head and open your mouth."

She heard his zipper, and when she rose his cock was placed perfectly so she could easily take him in her mouth. She opened her lips wide, her body quivering with delight. She loved the feel of his big cock stretching her jaws wide and filling her mouth. She loved his salty, musky flavor and the feel of his steely strength under the velvet skin, painted with a map of blue veins. Even his sac called to her lips, wanting to lave the crinkles and hear his groans of pleasure.

He didn't say a word, simply guided his hard length into her waiting mouth.

"Keep your hands behind your head and pleasure me, slave. I'll control the movement. You suck and lick."

There was no teasing or build up. He thrust his cock in and out of her mouth while she sucked and licked, her lips tightened around his wide girth. He grabbed her long hair and tugged her head so his cock would go in farther, his strokes speeding up as he neared orgasm. He bumped the back of her throat and she relaxed her jaw so she could take more of him. She wanted every inch, wanted him to feel pleasure as he had never known it before. His dick was shiny with her saliva and slid in and out effortlessly, rubbing against her already sensitive lips.

His fingers tightened painfully in her hair, adding to her arousal. His cock seemed to swell in her mouth and then he was coming, his hot seed spurting into her welcoming throat.

"Fuck, fuck. Every fucking drop, slave. Fuck."

She swallowed frantically, knowing missing even one drop was grounds for punishment. He tasted of Ian, of coffee, and something earthy she couldn't define. She sucked and licked until he was done, and then licked him clean, running her tongue up and down his cock and around the head and slit. He untangled his fingers from her hair and put himself back into his pants, zipping up. She let her eyes roam over his impressive figure. There was something about a man in a suit. Something commanding and masterful, and oh so very sexy.

"Good slave. Stand up, please."

She pushed herself up, getting more graceful each time she rose from her knees. She no longer looked like a tight-rope walker trying not to fall to the ground and break their neck.

"Place your hands behind your back and spread your legs a little wider."

She gratefully put her tired arms behind her back and spread her legs, a drop of her honey running down her thigh, tickling the sensitive flesh. He moved behind her and rubbed her fatigued shoulders, trailing his fingers in her hair so it hung down her back.

"Beautiful. You are so very beautiful, slave. Look in the mirror and tell me what you see. Tell me all the ways you are beautiful."

This was still hard for her. Her mother had always lectured her not to be vain. Looks were fine, but she shouldn't dwell on them. She'd been average size until after the twins were born. After that, it seemed both her mother and husband were constantly on her to lose weight. It had played havoc with her self-esteem. She had lost the weight, but inside she still felt like the woman who was never good enough. Now she was facing a huge mirror, butt naked, with a man who wanted her to tell him how she looked good.

She took a deep breath, uncomfortable with this activity. "My breasts are firm and round. Not too large and not too small."

Ian nodded. "Very true. They overflow my hand nicely. I love touching them and making the nipples hard. Continue."

"My skin is a nice color, and soft."

His hand glided down her arm, sending sparks to all her nooks and crannies. "Hmmmm, very soft, and the golden color is lovely. I love it when we are pressed close together, skin to skin. Continue."

She chewed her lip, rapidly running out of ideas. He silently waited, his hand stroking her back and hair. He wasn't going to let her off the hook.

"I have nice hair. It's wavy and thick, and it's a nice color."

His fingers combed through her hair, and he took some strands and tickled her nose. "Your hair is gorgeous, shiny and silky. I love to grab it when I'm fucking you from behind and tangle my fingers in it when you're sucking my cock. Continue, slave."

She couldn't think of another fucking thing. This entire exercise was starting to get on her nerves. She wasn't stupid. She knew what he was trying to do, but it was fucking annoying. She wasn't going to overcome a lifetime of insecurity with one session in front of a mirror. She pressed her lips together in frustration. He immediately recognized her mood and stepped back.

"Where are we, slave?"

"Yellow," she snapped. "Damn near red."

He nodded. "Then let's take a break and talk. Do you know why we're doing this, Tori?"

She gave him a look that would have singed the eyebrows off a lesser man.

"I'm not an imbecile. I have a genius IQ."

Why didn't he just pull her over his knee and spank her? She'd rather be whipped with a flogger than stand in front of this mirror and look at herself all damn day. He really was the devil.

"Yes, you're clearly a brilliant woman. I am trying to get you to see how beautiful you are and be less self-conscious. But I'm trying to show you something else, too."

She raised an eyebrow, in no mood for her Devil Dom's games.

He rested his hands on her shoulders, their weight and warmth beginning to drain her frustration. The things he could do with a simple touch amazed her.

"I'm trying to show you what I see when I look at you. I want you to see what makes me hard, what turns me on, what humbles me on a daily basis. I'm trying to get you to see you through my eyes. Maybe I should go about this another way."

She was trembling at his words, glad of his hands and arms touching and holding her. The look in his blue eyes was intense and passionate, and she wanted to lose herself in their depths. He ran his hands down her arms.

"Your body is worthy of worship. Your face is beautiful, the cheekbones high, and your mouth begs to be kissed. Your eyes are a deep shade of green with thick lashes. Your chin is stubborn. Very stubborn. You get a certain look on your face when you are digging your heels in. You had it when you told me we were at yellow."

His hands traveled to the top of her head. "This head houses a brilliant mind. I've never met a woman as smart or as funny. You have a quick sense of humor, and you get my stupid jokes."

His hands caressed her hair before brushing her ears. "You listen, really listen to me. You're not always staring at your phone or mesmerized with television. What I say is important to you, and you show me in so many ways."

His hands glided to her neck and shoulders.

"Your neck has a long line that beckons to my tongue. As I said before, your breasts are gorgeous. I could lick and play with them all night. Your nipples are a pretty pink and sensitive to my touch."

He brushed the already taut peaks with his callused fingers and she gasped with the contact. A zing of pleasure shot straight to her pussy. He pressed his hands over her heart.

"Your heart may be the best thing about you. It's soft and seems to have a limitless capacity for love and empathy. I've seen how you care about others. I've experienced how you care about me."

His fingers tickled her rib cage before settling on her hips.

"Your shape is womanly. Your hips made to fit the curve of my hand. Your stomach has faint silver lines from when you carried your sons. I know they were twins, and it amazes me how your body can go through something so miraculous. You made two human beings with hardly a sign left behind. How strong you must have had to be to go through it."

She blushed as he knelt next to her and traced the barely there stretch marks. She'd been only eighteen when she'd had her sons, and her skin had bounced back fairly well. Still, she'd always wished them away. Now, with him looking at her like she had done something no one else had ever done, she was proud of them. She'd earned those marks.

His hand cupped her bottom. "These ass cheeks are perfect for spanking. Their shape fits my palm exactly, as if they were made for one another. This ass is also perfect for fucking. Very soon, we're going to be together like that."

His questing fingers brushed her back hole and her body quivered in anticipation. She knew without a doubt she wanted his cock there. Everything he had done had brought her cascades of pleasure. She was sure this would be no different.

He moved his hands down to her thighs and nudged them apart.

"This pussy is mine. It belongs solely to me. It's wet and hot and feels like a perfect heaven when I'm inside you. I can't even begin to tell you how it feels when I'm fucking you. It's more pleasure than I've ever known. My cock fits so tight and snug in this cunt. It gets wet when I touch it, and it tastes like ambrosia. I love to lick your cream and make you come on my face."

He ran his hands up and down her legs, pressing tiny kisses to the inside of her thighs. She moaned with pleasure, her arousal building.

"These legs are strong and firm from your running and working out. When I'm inside you and you wrap them around my waist, it tells me you want to fuck as much as I do. These legs can also walk away from me or toward me. I always want you walking toward me, Tori."

He stood and turned her toward the mirror again. "This is what I see when I look at you."

She blinked and pressed her hands to her wet cheeks. She was crying, her tears running down her face. She'd never felt more beautiful than she did at this moment with this man. Her Devil Dom...with a soft, gooey center.

He brushed her hands away and wiped her tears, kissing the glistening trails on her cheeks.

"I didn't mean to make you cry, love. I just wanted to open your eyes. You're not only beautiful, you're smart and talented, a creative dynamo. You're a good friend, a good mother, and you're my woman."

She pressed herself against him and hugged him close. "You're my man. My Dominant."

Her heart ached in her chest. She was totally and completely in love with his man. Her throat was tight. The words wouldn't come. Actions would have to do. She dropped to her knees, her head bowed.

"Please, Master. Please let me serve you."

* * * *

"Yes, you may serve me. Stand, slave."

His voice was rough and gravelly, a lump in his throat. He'd loved other people in his life, his parents, his siblings, and his ex-wife. Nothing had prepared him for loving Tori Cordell. It filled every part of him and whipped him around until he was dizzy and drunk with happiness. He'd loved his ex-wife as a boy in his early twenties, as deeply as someone who hadn't truly experienced life, pain, joy, disappointment, and triumph could be expected to.

He loved Tori as a grown man with a man's heart and soul. It wasn't curable. He would love her until the day he died. He could only hope she felt the same, despite her earlier assertions she wasn't looking for permanence. The expression on her face shone bright with love. He simply couldn't be reading her wrong.

He moved her to the open area of his bedroom, her skin soft and fragrant. He leaned in and took a deep breath and the scent of sunshine and flowers teased his nostrils. He retrieved the cuffs he had hidden in his pocket and quickly buckled them around her wrists. He wanted to get to the good part. He knew exactly what scene they were going to play out tonight.

He reached up and grabbed one of the decorative chains from the hook in the wall. They were attached to a center hook in the ceiling, creating a canopy effect. The casual observer would think they were for show, an interior-design prop. They matched the gold chain pattern in the four-poster bed and caught the light when candles were lit. Only he knew they were for play time, and soon, so would Tori.

The hook in the ceiling was attached to a reinforced beam he had spent a few weekends installing. It would hold a hell of a lot more weight than Tori could put on it. The chain, while pretty, was actually quite strong and durable. He raised her arms above her head and clipped the cuffs to the chain, checking that her feet were firmly on the floor. He wanted her restrained but not uncomfortable.

He turned her body so she was facing the floor-to-ceiling mirror.

"Tonight, you'll watch yourself submit to me. I want you to see how beautiful and sexy your submission is."

This time she didn't try to turn away from her reflection. He stood back and took her in, her creamy skin almost pearlescent in the candlelight. His cock was hard and pressing against his zipper, ready for action. He ruthlessly pushed back his own needs. Bringing her to complete ecstasy came first.

He moved closer and pressed his lips to hers, tasting and teasing. Her eyes were already dark with passion, her lids heavy. He nipped at her bottom lip, soothing the hurt with his tongue.

He opened the bottom dresser drawer and pulled out a spreader bar with ankle cuffs attached. He held it up.

"This will hold your legs apart," he said as he attached each end. Her legs were now wide apart and she wouldn't be able to press her thighs together to stave off an orgasm.

He reached into the drawer again and pulled out a flogger, the long strands slapping against his thigh. He held it up for her inspection.

"This one is made of deer hide, very soft and supple. Kiss it, slave."

He held the handle in front of her lips, and she kissed it softly, her eyes never leaving his.

"Keep your gaze up and on me, slave. No looking down. Do you need to use your safeword?"

She shook her head, her long hair falling over her shoulder. "No, Master."

He set the flogger on top of the dresser and removed his jacket, his tie, and unbuttoned a few of the top buttons, before undoing the cuffs and rolling up his sleeves.

He reached for the flogger, slapping it against his thigh again, letting her know its power. He trailed the strands up and down her body, the candlelight throwing shadows on her curves. She shivered with every brush of the whip, her lips parted as she started to pant.

He pulled his arm back and gave her a soft-but-firm stroke with the strands. He continued whipping her softly, up and down her thighs and back, her skin rosy and flushed. He moved to her front and she thrust out her breasts for the fall of the flogger.

He didn't make her wait, sending the strands over her hard, pink nipples. She gasped with the sensation, letting her head fall back. He continued working her front, down her belly and finally to her thighs. Her splayed legs gave her pussy no protection from the whip, and she mewled in frustration when it only skimmed her cunt and clit.

"Look at yourself in the mirror, slave. Look how beautiful you are."

She did look beautiful. Her skin was pink from the flogger and covered in a fine sheen of perspiration. Her lips were swollen from his kisses and her thighs were shiny with her honey. She looked like a woman who was being well used by her Dom.

"Do you want more, slave? Where are we?"

Her bright moss-colored eyes glowed. "Please more, Master. I'm very green."

Chapter Ten

Every inch of her skin tingled where the flogger had stroked it. Her pussy clenched with arousal, needing his hard cock inside it. Her nipples were tight and begging for the flogger, his fingers, his tongue. Her clit, swollen and sensitive, needed the brush of the strands.

She arched her back, trying to invite his dominance. His arm went back and then the strands landed on her back, harder than before, the thud making a sound that sent cream pouring from her slit. The heat where it landed radiated out and she breathed heavily, her lids falling closed.

The whipping went on, each stroke sending her to heaven. She gave her body up to it, letting the pain and pleasure mix until her world had narrowed to only her, Ian, and the sensations he brought her.

He kept her guessing where the flogger would land, sometimes on the front of her thighs, sometimes on her ass, back, or breasts, and every now and then on her cunt, drawing a cry of pleasure from her. She was so close to the edge she could feel her orgasm shimmering in the distance. One firm snap of the strands on her clit and she would shatter. Instead, he held her on the edge, varying the intensity of each stroke. Light on her cunt and harder on her bottom.

Pleas for mercy fell from her dry lips. She was beyond caring about propriety or pride. She needed to come and she needed to come now.

"Please, Master! I need—I need—" She was panting, barely able to put sentences together, her arousal almost painful.

"I know what you need, slave. Come for me. Now."

The flogger came down with a snap once, twice on her vulnerable slit. She screamed as her orgasm took over. The waves shaking her, the pleasure so great it was overwhelming. She was grateful for the restraints as she was sure she would have crumpled to the ground in a heap from her climax. Lights danced in front of her eyes then finally faded away until he was holding her close, her heart pounding, her body limp.

"Good girl. You came hard for your Master. Let's get you down and on the bed."

He removed the spreader bar and unclipped her wrists from the chain, reaching under her knees and lifting her into his arms. She leaned against him, letting his scent surround her and the steady beat of his heart lull her into a calm, serene state. He laid her on the bed and stretched out next to her, holding her close and whispering silly things in her ear.

He pulled away and she reached for him instinctively. "Easy, love. I'm just taking my clothes off. I'll be right back for you."

She watched him shed his clothes, revealing his tan, muscular body. The golden hair and skin made him look a little like a Viking, and she smiled at the funny picture it made in her mind.

"What's the smile for, slave?"

She giggled. "You look like a Viking, Master. A golden Viking. So sexy."

"A Viking, huh? Then you're the Viking's slave. I'm going to ravish you as my prisoner."

She loved it when he was playful. He had a grin on his face and an enormous hard-on. What more could a girl ask for?

He climbed on top of her and pulled her arms over her head, attaching them to the headboard with the discreetly placed clip. He gave her an arrogant look worthy of any Nordic conqueror.

"Spread your legs, prisoner slave. I'm going to lick this pussy and taste your cream."

This was a command she could get behind. She pushed her thighs apart, making room for his wide shoulders. The first swipe of his tongue on her already-sensitized flesh made her toes curl. He explored every fold of her pussy, then tongue-fucked her hole. Honey gushed and she pulled at the restraints, wanting to hold his head in place. He lifted his head and raised an eyebrow.

"A prisoner doesn't usually get to come. Does this prisoner want an orgasm?"

She nodded vigorously. She was already teetering on the edge of a climax.

"Yes, please, Viking Master. I do want an orgasm."

He stroked his chin, his face stern, but his eyes twinkled. "Does the slave have anything to trade for this pleasure? What can you give me in return?"

She drew a fortifying breath. She wanted her actions to show him how she felt.

"My entire body, Viking Master, including my ass. Please take me there."

His eyebrows went up. She'd succeeded in surprising him.

"Is the prisoner sure this is what she wants to barter? Once I own your body, I will never let it go. It will be mine forever."

She smiled. "That's what I'm counting on."

His expression changed to one of raw desire. He nodded. "Your ass it is then. Turn over on your belly and get up on your knees."

The restraints allowed her to turn from her back to her belly and she tucked her knees under her, ass in the air. Her heart was pounding and she was starting to feel nervous. She wanted to do this but wondered how badly it would hurt.

His hand pushed back the hair from her face. "Relax, little slave. We're going to take this slow and gentle. Use 'yellow' if you need me to slow down and 'red' if you need me to stop completely. I don't say this often, so enjoy it. *You control this.*"

She let out a breath and relaxed. She trusted him to take care of her. She jumped when she felt the cold trickle of lube down her crack.

"Easy. I'm going to use my fingers to stretch you, just as I have in the past. Relax and go with it. You like this part, remember?"

She did like it. His fingers were brushing dark, naughty nerves that sent pleasure flowing through her body and straight to her clit. By the time he had three fingers inside her, she was moaning and wriggling her bottom, trying to get him deeper.

"I think you're ready for a cock."

He was gone for a moment to wash his hands and then she heard the crinkle of a condom. He leaned forward and held up a small syringe. The type used to give babies and toddlers their medicine.

"I've filled this with lube. I'm going to shoot this in your ass so you'll have lube all the way. It will make this first time easier."

She was all for making it easier. The head of the syringe went in and then she felt a rush of cold.

"Shit! That's cold."

Smack!

His hand came down on her ass cheek and she jumped from the contact. Immediately, the heat traveled to her burning pussy and clit. She loved her spankings.

"Watch your language, slave."

Hmmm…a spanking might be fun first.

"Don't tell me what to do, Ian. It was fucking cold."

His hands wound in her hair and he pulled her head back, his face stern.

"I know what you're doing, Tori. I do not tolerate topping from the bottom. As punishment, you will not receive a spanking, and you will wait for your pleasure until I orgasm. Not one minute before. I think a few more items will let you know who is in charge, too."

He was gone for a moment and then he was holding up a long strip of fabric and two nipple clamps with long chains attached.

"This is the other part of your punishment. I take topping from the bottom very seriously. I will not be manipulated. If you want something, you need to use your words and ask for it."

She swallowed the lump that had formed in her throat. She hated disappointing him.

"Yes, Master. I'm sorry."

He nodded. "Thank you for apologizing. I can see you are indeed sorry. I'm going to make sure the lesson is learned, however. Lift up as far as you can."

She lifted up as much as she could and he quickly attached the first clamp to her nipple. The long chain pooled on the bed. She hissed as the clamp tightened around her sensitive nipple. These hurt more than the last ones. He moved to the other side and repeated the process. He sat back on his heels and watched closely as she worked through the pain. Her perverse body took over and morphed the pain into heat and pleasure. Her clit throbbed and her pussy clenched. Hopefully, fucking was coming soon.

"Those are clover clamps. When I pull on these"—he held up the chain—"it will tighten the clamps. If I were you, I wouldn't move around too much when I'm fucking you. I'll have these in my hands while I'm inside you."

A gush of honey followed his words. If any other man in the world had dared to do these things to her she would have kicked him hard in the balls. What was it about this man that had her nipples aching and her cunt crying out for cock?

He picked up the black strip of fabric and wound it around her head, fastening it so she couldn't see.

"The blindfold will heighten your senses. I don't want you to miss a moment of the nipple clamps or my cock in your ass because you're distracted by something else."

He bent close to her ear and she felt his warm breath on her neck. "Are you beginning to see why I'm called the Devil Dom, pretty slave?"

She nodded. "Yes, Master. But you're *my* Devil Dom, so it's okay."

He chuckled. "I do belong to you, don't I? There's no denying it.

You belong to me, too. I wish you could see yourself right now. Restrained, blindfolded. Your nipples clamped and your thighs shiny with your cream. You want this, don't you, Tori?"

"Yes, Master. I want this."

He kissed a wet path down her spine. "Where are we, slave?"

"Green, Master."

"Good girl. We'll start out vanilla."

Tori wasn't sure what part of any of this was vanilla, but she felt his cock pressing into her cunt and all rational thought fled. He was holding the chains to the clamps like reins on a horse and tried to keep her body still as he impaled her on his thick, long cock. She groaned as he seated himself to the hilt.

"Do you like cock, slave? Tell me what you want."

She was breathing heavy, her cunt tightening on his dick. "I love your cock, Master. Fuck me, please."

"I love your pussy. The way it sucks me in and feels so hot and wet." His voice sounded gravelly. He was as aroused as she was.

He pulled out and thrust back in, hard, sending frissons of pleasure all the way to her fingertips and toes. He fucked her slowly, each stroke hard but measured, making her crazy for more. She arched her back and tried to press against him, urging him to go faster, but he tightened the chains and the clamps bit into her poor nipples, making the point of who was firmly in charge. He kept up the easy pace, serious about making her wait for her pleasure.

She cried out when he pulled completely out of her pussy. He patted her bottom and then pressed into her tight back hole. None of the plugs had been quite as large as his cock, plus this was hot, pulsating flesh, not impersonal, lubricated plastic. She groaned as the tight ring of muscles gave way and the head of his cock was inside. He moved the chains to his left hand and grasped her hip tightly with his right.

"Where are we, slave?"

"Green, Master." Her voice sounded weak and strained.

"Are you sure? Do we need to take a minute?"

She shook her head. She needed him to move. "No! Please, I need more."

"You are not green, Tori. Take some deep breaths for me and relax."

She took a couple of deep breaths, his soft voice whispering encouragement in her ear. When she was calm, he kissed her shoulder.

"Now you are green. Push out for me."

She pushed against his cock while he pressed forward slowly. She couldn't see him, but she could hear his ragged breath. He was holding himself in control, fighting his animal instinct to thrust into her hard, regardless of the consequences. He grabbed her other hip and steadied her as he thrust in the last few inches.

His cock was deeply embedded in her ass and she wasn't sure she liked it.

"Yellow, Master. Yellow."

"We'll stay just this way until you're ready. You're in control of this one. Just breathe, Tori."

She let herself go limp, letting her mind drift somewhere. Her nipples stung and her ass was stretched so she couldn't go far. She was surprised when the urge to move overtook the uncomfortable feeling of being split in two. She fidgeted restlessly.

"Green, Master. I need you to move. I need to feel something."

He seemed to understand and began a slow, steady fucking. With each thrust, he groaned with pleasure. Tori was panting, his cock starting to rub those naughty nerves he'd woken up with his fingers. Pleasure was starting to build in her cunt and clit. She wanted to come badly.

Her fingers grabbed the sheets and held tightly, her body jolted with every stroke of his hard dick in her ass. She spread her thighs a little wider to get more traction to meet his thrusts more fully, but he pulled her back to her original position.

"No, slave. You won't come until I do. Where are we?"

She gritted her teeth in frustration. Punishments sucked. At least this one did. She swayed her ass to get more contact, but he simply pulled on the chains to her burning nipples and held her hips tighter, his hands biting into the flesh.

"Where are we, slave?" His voice was dark and deep and she had to obey him.

"Green, you Devil asshole. Green. I need to come!"

"You're not even done with this punishment and you're racking up more. Your next one is going to be even more unpleasant than this one, I can promise you. You'll wait for your orgasm, naughty slave. You'll wait even longer now."

She was already in trouble. She let go a string of expletives that would have made a trucker blush. Her evil Dom's reaction was typical. He just laughed and slowed down his thrusts.

"Someday you're going to learn I am in charge, slave."

It looked like that day was going to be today.

* * * *

Damn, if this feisty sub wasn't testing his control. He needed to make her wait for her orgasm, but all he wanted to do was let go and climax himself. These long, slow strokes in her tight ass were sending him over the edge, and he had to fight to keep from exploding.

He chuckled to himself. His little slave was in big trouble. He wasn't sure what her punishment was going to be yet, but the next scene they had was going to be a punishment scene. He couldn't do anything more to her tonight—her body could only take so much—but he would take great pleasure in planning it out over the next few days and reminding her often of the impending discipline. The sheer dread and anticipation could be part of her correction.

His body was bathed in sweat and he sped up his thrusts. He couldn't hold out much longer. He felt the pressure building in his balls, and his cock ached. Time for the clamps to come off. He reached around and pulled one off and then other as quickly as he could. She screamed as the blood rushed back into her nipples. He rubbed her clit and her ass clamped down on his cock. He groaned as he let go, his orgasm tearing him into pieces at the same time hers tore through her body.

His whole body jerked in rhythm with his cock jetting out his seed. His vision blurred and the room seemed to tilt before righting itself. He was worn out, slumped over his slave. They were both covered in sweat and sticky from her honey and the lube.

He reached forward and unclipped her hands from the headboard, removed the blindfold, and with fumbling fingers unbuckled her cuffs. He pulled from her body slowly, both of them groaning as they separated.

"I'll be right back, sweetheart. I need to take care of the condom."

He disposed of the condom in the trash and started to run them a bath. A soak in the tub would help Tori's sore muscles and be a nice relaxing place for aftercare.

He stretched out on the bed next to her, tucking an errant strand of her dark hair behind her ear.

"You were amazing, love. How about a bath?"

He levered up from the bed, but she grabbed his arm, a strange look on her face. He panicked for a moment, wondering if she was hurt or disgusted. He started to speak, but she pressed her fingers to his lips.

"I tried to say this earlier when we were in front of the mirror, but I couldn't get the words out. If I don't say them now, I don't know when I'll be able to work up the courage again."

She dropped her hand and smiled. "I love you, Ian Taggert. I've only said that to my parents, my husband, and my sons. Now, I've said it to you. It's a big deal for me. I didn't expect, or even really want, to fall in love. But here I am, ass over tea kettle as Lisa puts it, over a Devil Dom. I love you."

Her words took his breath away. This amazing woman loved him. She loved him. He wasn't perfect by a long stretch. He was basically a normal guy, nothing special about him except his sexual proclivities, which could have driven her away. Instead he felt this miraculous joy in his heart. He cupped her jaw, overcome with so many emotions. Love, yes, but even more elation, gratitude, relief, and a hunger to spend every moment of the rest of their lives together.

"Tori Cordell, if you think I'm not ass over tea kettle in love with you, you're mistaken. I love you so damn much I can't even find the words. You're everything to me. Mostly, you're my future. I've never felt like this before. I love you."

She knocked him back on the bed as she launched herself at him, kissing and laughing. He swung her up in his arms and carried her toward the bathroom, lowering her into the steaming bath water. A sigh escaped her pink lips as she relaxed in the water.

"Sorry, I didn't have any bath beads or whatever you women like to use. It's just water, but it should help with any soreness. Relax in the tub. I'm going to get you something to drink. Water for dehydration and wine to celebrate. What do you think?"

She stretched her legs and smiled up at him, a mischievous gleam in her eye. "I like the wine part." She pointed toward the door. "Get my wine, slave boy. I'm thirsty."

He quirked his eyebrow. "I'll add that to your growing list of transgressions to be punished for. You're mighty brave, lady."

She gave him a dreamy smile. "You love me."

He headed for the kitchen. "I damn sure do, but it doesn't mean I won't punish you. Quite the opposite, in fact."

He whistled a tune as he grabbed the wine and glasses, along with a bottle of water. He had a lifetime to think of dastardly, erotic punishments for his beautiful little slave.

* * * *

"This wine is delicious." Tori leaned back onto Ian's chest, stretching her legs out and placing one on the side of the bathtub. She felt languorous after their lovemaking, and soaking in the steaming water was a good place to relax afterward. Ian had even brought in some candles from the bedroom and chocolate cake to nibble on. She was in heaven.

"It's a California merlot. I'm not just a dumb cop, you know. I can pair wine with chocolate."

His chuckle vibrated in his chest. "You certainly can. Dark-chocolate truffle cake and red wine. You could join our book club."

"I think I'll pass. Too much estrogen for me."

She sipped her wine and set it on the edge of the tub before grabbing his hand and tracing patterns on his palm.

"You said you loved me earlier."

"That I did, beautiful." She could hear the smile in his voice.

"You also said you'd never felt this way before." She hesitated, not sure she wanted to open this can of worms. They'd never really talked about it before. "But you were married before."

Ian levered up in the water, taking her with him. He turned her so she was looking into his warm blue eyes.

"I was married. Sherry and I got married right out of college. She's a good woman, and we were pretty happy for a few years. We simply married too young. We woke up one day staring thirty in the face and realized our lives had simply grown apart. We loved each other, but we weren't in love with each other. Fuck, we'd turned into roommates. Casual and friendly but no fire."

She waved her hand, embarrassed she had been so insecure she needed to ask. "You don't have to explain anymore."

He grabbed her shoulders and gave her a little shake. "Yes, I do. I guess I should have talked about this before, but hell, it was a long time ago. I've been divorced for five years. I care about Sherry, and she and I are still good friends. She's remarried and has a couple of kids. We didn't have one of those nasty divorces or anything like that.

It was friendly. Shit, maybe too friendly. I play golf with her new husband sometimes."

"Is he a Dom, too?"

Ian shook his head and laughed. "That would be a resounding fuck no. Sherry hated the lifestyle and only dabbled in submission to make me happy. The more I immersed myself in becoming a Dominant, the more she went her own way. It was one, just one, of the things we realized we didn't have in common. My being a cop was another. She hated being married to a cop. Hated the hours, working on holidays, the supposed danger, everything. She married a dentist."

Laughter bubbled up. "A dentist? That's a pretty safe profession unless someone bites your hand."

"Being a detective is pretty safe. Hell, most of my time I feel like I just push paper."

She grabbed his hands and wrapped her own around them. "Thank God. I know how she felt. If anything happened to you, I don't know what I'd do."

"I'm not going anywhere, Tori. I wouldn't ask you to go through what you've already gone through a second time."

He was talking about the death of her husband.

She nodded. "I know you wouldn't. There are no guarantees about how long we'll all be here. I've learned we have to appreciate what we have now."

He lifted their entwined fingers and kissed her hands. "What we have now is pretty amazing. I want you to move in, Tori. I don't want us to waste any time. I want us to start appreciating what we have now."

Her heart felt like it was going to pound its way out of her chest. "I want that, too. I'm not sure what we're going to do about the boys, though."

Ian grinned, pulling her close, the water sloshing onto the tiled floor. "The boys can stay at your house and you can live here. We're close enough to keep an eye on them and still give them some privacy and independence. They're getting older and becoming men."

They were becoming men. Good men. They knew she was dating, and soon they would know she was in love. She hoped they would understand and learn to love Ian, but she wouldn't be scared away if they had issues. It was time she started living for herself. In a few years, the boys would be on their own and she would be alone. She deserved a life and happiness, too. Time to grab that happiness with both hands.

She grinned at the thought and giggled. Tori knew what to grab first. She slid her hands down his torso and grabbed his quickly hardening cock with greedy fingers.

"I think we should start the whole 'not wasting time' thing right now. I want to appreciate you."

He leaned back in the tub, hands behind his head. "Honey, you can appreciate me all night."

They appreciated each other until the bath water was ice cold and sloshed all over the bathroom. They donned robes and ate a quiet dinner in the living room, watching a football game on television and snuggling. Tori had never been happier. She had a brand-new future to look forward to.

Chapter Eleven

Tori muttered to herself in frustration. She needed to get dinner started, but instead she was in her backyard fussing with the yard work. She finally sighed and dropped the gardening gloves on the patio table. The sun was going down. She wasn't going to get any more done today. Tomorrow was another day, and now she was looking for a shower and a glass of wine while she threw some steaks on the grill. Ian should be home in an hour or so, and he always came home hungry.

She put away the yard tools in her garage and locked her backdoor before crossing the twenty-five feet to Ian's house. She still couldn't believe she'd fallen in love with the boy next door.

Okay, the Dom next door.

It was fate, no doubt about it. She couldn't wait until Thanksgiving so her boys could meet Ian and he could meet her boys. Maybe she was naive, but she was hoping for one big happy family.

She pushed open his sliders into the kitchen and headed straight for the refrigerator. She needed a glass of water before she needed anything else. It was still hot in Florida even in November, but luckily the humidity was giving her a break. Maybe she could convince Ian to have a midnight swim in her pool tonight. A romantic moonlight swim.

She was engrossed in her own thoughts of their bodies floating through silky, cool water when a hand wound around her face and covered her mouth. The other arm dragged her to the floor, pressing her to the cool tile. She kicked and scratched at the intruder, determined to hurt him as much as he planned to hurt her. She bit at the glove, trying to dislodge his hand from her mouth and jaw. She managed to get his hand to slip and twist around so she was facing him. She screamed at the top of her lungs before he landed a hard backhand punch to her face.

She was dizzy and her ears were buzzing as he started to grab at her clothes. He was dressed in jeans and a hoodie again, pulled low so she couldn't see his face. Her mind went into survival mode. He wasn't a big man, but his body was straddling hers, holding her prisoner, and making her feel trapped.

She raked at his hands with her nails and brought her knee up as hard as she could to his groin. He fell back on his heels with a groan, and she grabbed at the hoodie and pulled it away, determined to scratch and punch at his face. She vaguely remembered seeing something on television about using the heel of her hand to break her attacker's nose. To break it, she needed to see it.

She wrestled the hoodie off his head as he held his balls. What she saw took her breath away and she froze, unable to comprehend the identity of her attacker.

Detective Tim Mills, Ian's partner.

* * * *

Ian stretched his shoulders and yawned, heading to his car. He'd worked twelve hours today on surveillance of The Boyfriend's intended victim and not a fucking thing happened. Then, he'd let Tim talk him into letting him leave early and Ian doing the daily surveillance report. Apparently, Tim was headed out for some hook-up with a woman. Now it was late, Tim was probably getting laid, Ian was tired and hungry, and Tori would probably be wondering where the hell he was.

Not that she would call him to find out. Tori had this thing about no nagging and no hunting him down when he was running late. When she'd told him she wouldn't do that, he'd been skeptical. In his experience, women loved to nag men about every little thing and loved to keep tabs on them. Making sure they toed the line, so to speak.

Tori eschewed all those things. She simply smiled and told him she'd seen women who nagged, and it appeared to her the husbands of those women stopped listening to their wives. Therefore, when the women really did have a legitimate complaint the husbands had already stopped hearing their women. Consequently, she said if she did complain to him, he should take it seriously because she wasn't going to complain about every little thing.

She also was going to treat him like the big boy he was and not constantly call him at work, bugging him about what he was in the mood to eat for dinner and when was he planning to be home. Tori was too mature of a woman for playing those games. She'd looked at him smugly and explained she had an interesting life of her own. She didn't need to horn in on his. She trusted he would come home when he said he would and call when he couldn't.

Simple. Straightforward. No bullshit head games.

Damn, but he loved her. It had only been yesterday they'd exchanged I love yous, but he was already thinking about the future. He wanted a ring on her finger and a collar around her neck.

He stuck the key in the ignition and tried to start the car, but the engine wouldn't turn over. Nothing seemed to work, and it just made a clicking sound every time he turned the key.

Fuck.

He wouldn't be getting home any time soon. It looked like his battery was dead. He headed back into the station to find some jumper cables. His last set was in Tori's car after she'd left her lights on accidentally in the mall parking lot. He'd had various sets through the years, and somehow they seemed to migrate from his car to the cars of his friends.

He waved to his coworker Detective Patrick O'Malley, who was exiting the building. "Hey, Pat. My car battery is dead. You got a set of jumper cables? Tori has my set in her car."

Pat laughed. "My wife has my set, too." He pointed to a row of file cabinets against the wall. "I remember Tim had a set in his drawer of the file cabinet."

"Thanks."

Every detective had their own drawer in the three file cabinets lining the far wall. Since case files were kept in central filing, they all joked the drawers were for storing gin bottles and snacks.

He pulled open the drawer and started to rummage through the contents. He didn't see the jumper cables, and he started pulling some of the items out of the drawer in case they were at the bottom. A file folder filled with photos opened and its contents spilled on the floor, making Ian sigh in exasperation. He bent down to retrieve them and looked at them in disbelief. There were photos of the first five victims of The Boyfriend, clearly taken prior to their assaults, as they were pretty beat-up after the attacks.

Ian's heart pounded, and he wracked his brain for a reason for these to be in Tim's drawer. Had there been letters Ian didn't know about? If so, why weren't these locked away in evidence?

He scraped his hand down his face in grim determination. He started digging through the contents again, finding a tablet of paper that looked very much like the paper The Boyfriend letters had been written on. Ian felt sick to his stomach as he read the notes, written in the same handwriting as their perpetrator.

The tablet had papers folded and stuffed in the back, and Ian pulled them out and unfolded the one on top. It was a Google map of Ian's own neighborhood, his house clearly visible. But it wasn't his own house on the map that made the blood drain from his face.

Tim had circled Tori's house.

Everything fell into place. Tim's enthusiasm about being famous and on the news. The Boyfriend had the same obsession. The Boyfriend talked about the next victim being in their own backyard, their own neighborhood. He hadn't meant his neighborhood. He'd meant Ian's. They'd been playing this all wrong.

Fuck. Shit. Fuck.

When he'd said he wanted her the most, he hadn't been talking about the girl in the picture. He'd been talking about the girl in Ian's neighborhood. The girl in the picture was a red herring.

I am so fucking stupid. I introduced them.

He grabbed his cell and called Tori. The phone rang but no one answered. She always answered her phone. He grabbed Pat, who had come back into the building to make sure Ian was able to get home.

"I know who The Boyfriend is, and I think I know where he is. Call every unit we've got. We have to stop him before he hurts Tori."

* * * *

"Why? For the love of God, why?"

Tim didn't answer, only grimaced and then smirked. He grabbed her wrists and pinned them over her head, leaning forward, his weight once again pinning her to the hard tile floor.

"I'm going to be famous. You weren't supposed to see it was me, you stupid bitch."

Tori didn't like being called names, and she really didn't like this asshole's grip on her wrists. It wasn't the least arousing, like when Ian did it. It simply fucking hurt and it was pissing her off. She was going to give him the fight of her life.

She brought up her knee and tried to knee him again, but he used his legs to pin her thighs to the floor. She was held flat on the tile, but he was as incapacitated. He had to use practically his entire body to hold her down.

He pulled one hand from her wrists and grabbed her already sore jaw.

"If you stop struggling, it won't hurt so bad."

She doubted he had any real regard for her feelings. But trying to reason with him seemed like a good idea. Maybe she could talk her way out of this.

"I don't want you to hurt me, Tim. I'm a mother, you know. I have two sons."

His eyes narrowed, and she could swear she saw a flicker of uncertainty there.

"My mother is going to be proud of me. My dad, too."

Her heart was pounding so loud she was surprised he didn't hear it. She swallowed hard and tried to even her breathing.

"I'm sure they're already proud of you. Didn't you make detective quite young?"

A cocky grin spread across his face and his grip loosened slightly on her wrists. "I did. I'm a genius. Criminals are stupid, but I'm not. I've had the entire police department chasing their tails. They have no clue who The Boyfriend is. I even gave myself the nickname. I thought it up in advance."

His face was more animated, and his grip loosened a little more. She wouldn't need much more and she could pull her hands out of his grip and either go for his nose or eyes.

"It's a very good nickname. It's too bad the newspapers couldn't write about it."

His expression turned to anger in an instant. "That was Ian's call. He wanted to keep some of the details a secret. I had to go along with it since he was the *senior* detective." He practically spat out the last two words.

"They should have let you have your way." She kept her voice low and soothing as if she was talking to a spooked horse. She tried to move one of her wrists mere millimeters, hoping he was too caught up in his own emotions to notice.

He didn't blink an eye, still angry about the injustices he'd endured at Ian's hands. "We had to do everything Ian's way. Like he was a fucking god or something. He's not right all the time. He can be wrong."

His hold became much looser, his grip barely grazing her skin.

His body had lifted slightly and his weight wasn't as heavy.

"When I saw you with him that day at the bar, I knew I had to have you. It was the perfect 'fuck you' to Mr. Perfect Detective. I was going to have his woman and he'd never figure it out. I even sent him a letter giving him a clue and he still didn't know it was me."

He sat up, his hands abandoning her arms, his face a scowl. She inched her arms down until they were by her head, ready to attack.

"Eventually, I would have found someone to take the blame for all of this. Planted some evidence and been the hero. I can't do that now."

"I won't tell anyone."

He leaned forward, his hands on either side of her chest. "I know you won't. I'll make sure of it."

She couldn't wait any longer. She flung both hands forward and scraped her nails down his face, gouging in as far as she could. He howled in pain, his hands catching her forearms and forcing them to the floor. She kicked and struggled to get him off of her, knowing it was her only chance. Long trails of blood were dripping from his face, and his eyes had gone cold. She went limp and he seemed thrown off by the action. She took her advantage and twisted to her side, taking him with her so he wasn't on top anymore. Now it was a wrestling match with an injured man for her freedom and her life.

She was running out of steam and not sure she could fight him off when she heard the sirens. They were coming loud and fast, and she breathed a sigh of relief when they stopped in front of the house.

She heard the sound of running feet and then the front door burst open and cops poured in, pulling Tim off of her and slapping him into handcuffs. She slumped against the cabinets, breathing hard, every bone in her body hurting. Suddenly, Ian was crouched beside her, lifting her into his arms and carrying her outside.

She pressed on his shoulder. "I'm okay. I'm okay, Ian."

His jaw was tight and his skin a ghastly shade of gray. "No, you're not. You need to go to the hospital, and I'm going with you.

I'm going to let the other guys take Tim in. If I see him, I'm going to fucking kill him."

He lay her down on a stretcher and the paramedics started checking her vital signs.

"How did you know it was him? How did you know he was after me?"

"It's a long story, love. I'll tell you everything as soon as we get you fixed up. Oh, and the front door of your house was kicked down. I sent cops to both houses just in case."

They were loading her into an ambulance. "I'll forgive you if you tell me now."

Ian stepped in after her leaning down to whisper in her ear, "You've already got several punishments coming to you from your previous transgressions. Do you want to add one more by questioning your Dom when it comes to your safety and well-being?"

He looked totally fucking serious. She remembered their first conversation about a Dominant submissive-relationship and how he'd made a point he had the final word when it came to her health and safety. She'd agreed to it.

She shook her head, the ambulance doors closing. "No, I already have too many coming to me. I don't want anymore."

"Good call, Tori. Let's get you to the hospital and I'll explain everything when we're done."

* * * *

"You promised to tell me the whole story."

Ian's house was a crime scene, so they were at Tori's house. She'd had a soothing bath, fresh pajamas, a bowl of soup, ice packs for her bruises, and a prescription painkiller. Ian had chosen a glass of wine to end his day. She was already sleepy, but she was determined to hear the entire story.

She knew Ian had talked to the cops who had transported Tim

Mills to the station. Tim had talked quite a bit while Tori had been treated at the hospital, wanting everyone to know the injustice he had suffered and how life wasn't fair. Tori had also given her statement to Detective Patrick O'Malley, detailing everything Tim had said to her in Ian's kitchen.

He lifted her onto his lap and pressed a brief kiss to her lips. "I keep my promises. I'm just not sure where to start."

She laid her head on his chest, listening to the steady beat of his heart and feeling the warmth of his body. "Start at the beginning. Is Tim crazy?"

"Perhaps. He'll have a psychological examination. If I were to guess from what I know and what you said he talked about, he is probably a sociopath, maybe with narcissistic tendencies. I'm no profiler. I took just enough psychology to do my job."

"You do your job well. You showed up in the nick of time."

His jaw tightened. "I should have fucking figured it out before tonight. He gave me clues. I just didn't see them for what they were. It never occurred to me a fellow cop would be behind this. He counted on that."

"He obfuscated everything. You can't blame yourself. You did figure it out." She ran her hand up and down his chest, trying to soothe him. He was angry at himself, and he shouldn't be. He'd saved her, after all.

"The beginning, remember?" she prompted.

He let out a sigh. "He came up with a plan to get a promotion and get his face on the news and in the papers. He would commit these crimes, set someone else up, then take credit for apprehending them. Apparently, he had it all figured out."

Ian sipped his wine, his expression grim. "When he didn't get as much publicity as he wanted, he started sending me letters to stir up interest, hoping the station would go public with them. Of course, we didn't. He wanted to taunt us, me specifically with a picture of his next victim."

"The first picture? She was his next victim wasn't she?"

He nodded. "Yes. At that point, he hadn't met you. Once he met you, his goal changed. He was wildly attracted to you, and he wanted to hurt me. He decided to go after you. In the letter, he said he wanted you the most, then included a picture of some waitress from a cops bar as a diversion."

"She's the one you've been watching?"

He snorted. "Fat lot of good it did us. She wasn't his intended victim. He only wanted me busy and distracted. Tonight, he unhooked the battery cables in my car so it wouldn't start and it would slow me down in getting home. He thought I would call the auto club. Instead, I asked for jumper cables."

Tori chuckled. "Shit, they're in my car."

Ian took another sip of wine and placed the glass on the end table. "Thank God those jumper cables were in your car. I asked Pat, the detective who took your statement, if he had any and he said he didn't but Tim had some in his file drawer. That's where I found all the evidence. Somewhere, deep down, he may have wanted to be caught. Everything was where anyone at all could have found it. There's no privacy at the station house."

She shuddered. "Have they searched his home yet? Had he targeted any other women after me?"

"So far, they've found several photos of other women and letters to me already written and ready to post. They also found a rose in the front seat of his car. It was parked a few blocks away from here. He must have been so excited to get to you he forgot to bring his calling card."

"The book club is so not going to believe this."

Ian laughed and wrapped his arms around her, lifting her up easily and heading to the bedroom. "That's your worry? Whether your friends are going to believe what happened? I think the medication is starting to mess with you. Time for bed."

He pulled back the covers and placed her gently on the mattress.

"It's over, love. Time to get some sleep."

She grabbed his arm. "You're going to sleep next to me, aren't you?"

He slid in next to her. "I wouldn't sleep anywhere else."

She stared into his eyes for a moment. "You know what the weirdest thing about all this is?"

He pulled her close and reached for the light. "What is weird, honey?"

"Tim got exactly what he wanted. His name is on the news and in the paper. He's famous."

The light went out and the room was plunged into darkness except for the moonlight streaming in the window. It was a full moon tonight. She'd heard a full moon made people do crazy, stupid things.

"Hell of a thing to be famous for. I think I'll stay an anonymous police detective."

"And Devil Dom," she added, almost asleep.

His arms tightened around her, his masculine scent surrounding her.

"Uh uh, not just any Devil Dom. I'm your Devil Dom. Sleep, baby. You're going to need your rest." He kissed her temple. "You have a couple of punishments coming."

She heard him chuckle and she felt his warm breath on her shoulder. She felt safe and warm and let her body drift to sleep, knowing he would always be there to hold her in his arms.

Chapter Twelve

"Whatever Master wishes."

Tori giggled as they entered the foyer of The Estate. Four days had passed since Tim Mills had been caught, and they'd been filled with police statements, Ian working long hours, and her bruises and face healing. Her jaw still looked like she had run into a wall, but the bruises on her body had already started to fade. She wanted to put the whole thing firmly behind her, and what better way than a play party at The Estate? She convinced Ian this was what both of them needed.

"Don't try that with me, Tori," Ian all but growled. He was frustrated with her, it was clear. She already knew she had punishments coming. Making him a little crazy probably wouldn't make them much worse.

Besides, she was frustrated, too. Sexually frustrated. Her Dom was a stubborn man. He refused to have sex with her until she was "healed," whatever that meant.

She'd been teasing him in the car all the way here. One look at Ian's face told her he was one pissed-off Dominant. She was so going to get a spanking tonight.

"You've been pushing me all night. Fuck, you've been pushing me for the last three days. This is going to be one long night for you. I may, I repeat, may, let you come at the end of the evening. We'll see. It depends on how well you take your discipline. In the meantime, don't bother begging. It won't have any effect on me."

Uh oh. I've poked the Devil Dom too much, maybe.

"Um, I'm sorry, Master?" She peeked up at him through her lashes, wondering if perhaps she had gone too far.

He shook his head, his expression stern. "Too little, too late, brat. I think this will be an evening you won't forget for awhile."

That sounded ominous. She knew he'd never really hurt her, but she realized he was absolutely going to punish her tonight. Her only choice was using her safeword.

He clipped her wrist cuffs together behind her back and attached a leash to her collar, giving it a tug. She still wasn't a fan of the leash but she loved the outfit she had on tonight. It was a black silk thong, a corset, and black high heels with little bows at the back. The corset was white satin with a covering of black lace. It nipped in her waist and pushed up her breasts, and she adored the way she looked in it. Ian, however, had barely glanced at it, seemingly lost in his own thoughts.

Ian led her deeper into The Estate, farther than they had gone the last time she'd been here. Finally, they entered a dimly lit room with candles everywhere. It looked like an opulent dungeon with comfortable overstuffed chairs and couches, a bar, a large four-poster canopy bed, and several devices of torture, including a St. Andrew's cross, a bondage table, and a spanking bench.

He led her into the center of the room, and she started to get nervous. There were already people in the room, and as she looked closely, she realized the people were her friends.

Holy shit, is that Noelle?

Ian pointed to the floor and she sank to her knees while Conor, Nate, Jeremy, Cole, and Cam all stood up. Sara, Lisa, Brianne, and Noelle were all kneeling on cushions, wearing beautiful fetish wear and big smiles. Had her Devil Dom invited her friends to witness her discipline? And were they happy about it? That was mean.

Conor and Cam walked up to Ian. Cam put his hand on Ian's shoulder. "Are we ready to begin?"

Ian nodded and Cam cleared his throat, addressing the room.

"We are gathered here today to witness an offering. In every relationship, each person has something very precious to give the other." He paused and gave Noelle a tender smile. Noelle practically glowed as she smiled back, her eyes full of love. "Today, this Dominant, Ian Taggert, is offering this submissive, Tori Cordell, his love, devotion, protection, and care. The symbol of this offering is a collar. A collar in our community can mean many things. Tonight, this collar means a lifetime commitment. Ian, do you have a collar to offer this submissive?"

Tori's heart was pounding out of her chest, and she could barely breathe. She wasn't being punished after all. She was being offered forever. She felt tears prick her eyes and tried to blink them away. Her Devil Dom had gathered her friends together so she could share this moment with them.

Ian nodded and pulled something from his pocket. It sparkled in the candlelight.

Cam looked down at her. "This Dominant wishes to offer you a collar. Do you wish to accept this collar and all that it represents?"

She nodded, her throat tight. "Yes, I do, Sir."

Cam smiled and turned to Ian. "Place the collar around her neck and make your solemn vow."

Ian held up the necklace and then placed it around her neck, the clasp snapping in place. No one would ever know it was her collar. It looked like a regular necklace, almost a choker type, with a diamond heart nestled between her collarbones. She loved the feel of it, the weight of it on her neck.

Ian caressed her uninjured jaw. "I promise to care for and protect you, putting your needs above my own. I promise to give you what you need, not just what you want. I promise to keep you safe, your health and well-being a priority in my life. I promise to be strong and responsible, a Dominant and a man you can count on and respect. I promise to do what I say I will do. I promise to be consistent and fair. I promise to listen to not only what you say but what you don't say. I promise to respect the gift of your submission. I promise to love you every day of my life. This is my solemn vow."

Cam looked back at her. "If you wish, Tori, you may also make a solemn vow to your Dominant."

She nodded and took a breath. She wasn't prepared, so she let her heart speak for her. "I promise to give myself to you, both my body and my heart. I promise to devote myself to putting your needs first, before my own. I promise to respect the gift of your dominance, knowing you will keep me safe. I promise to trust you. I promise to love you every day of my life. This is my solemn vow." Her voice choked a little at the end. She was overcome with emotion and the beauty of the ceremony.

"A collar represents a sacred bond between the Dominant and submissive," Conor said. "It's a bond the vanilla world may not understand or accept, but it runs deep and true. Ian and Tori have invited us here today to not only witness their bond, but to celebrate our own. Would anyone, Dominant or submissive, like to speak about the sacred connection they share?"

Noelle raised her hand. "The necklace you wear was designed and crafted by myself. As I was designing it, I thought about the journey of a Dominant and submissive. Each link in the collar represents a step in your coming together. The heart represents the love that is the center of your relationship. The clasp is the trust which is the cement which holds everything together. Always put your relationship first, before anything else. It will grow and flourish."

"Thank you," Tori mouthed silently.

Conor smiled. "Thank you, Noelle. Those are wise words. Anyone else?"

Lisa raised her hand. "Submission is not about weakness. It's about strength. Weak people cannot submit. It takes someone strong to give everything they are to another human being. There is also a peace that comes from this gift. It's a peace I crave, and a sanctuary for me. Never let others make you feel less because you submit."

A tear rolled down Tori's cheek. Lisa's eyes were filled with tears, also. In fact, every woman in the room looked about to cry.

Brianne raised her hand. "Submission has led me to a deeper trust and devotion to my husband. I feel like he really knows and understands me. He accepts me as I am. That's a gift I never thought I would have."

Conor looked at Sara, but she shook her head, wiping a tear from her cheek. She and her husbands only played at the lifestyle, so Tori was surprised when Jeremy spoke. "I'm not a Master, and neither is Cole, although Sara would probably tell you we're bossy as all hell." A wave of laughter ran through the room. "I do want to say that we love this woman with all our heart and soul. She trusts us, delights us, and loves us. We're truly blessed."

Sara threw her arms around her men, and Conor smiled indulgently.

"I'll go next," Nate said. He placed his hand on Brianne's head, stroking her auburn hair. "I'm humbled by the trust this woman has placed in me. I'm humbled by her love. Her capacity to give and care is limitless. One lifetime isn't enough with her."

Conor cleared his throat. "I guess it's my turn." He looked at Lisa kneeling on the floor. "This journey with Lisa has been far from easy but always worth it. We started out as two kids having fun and exploring our kinky side. It became a lifestyle for us, and something I've never regretted. It's brought us closer and helped me see what an amazing woman Lisa is. My wife is a formidable woman. It takes a strong woman to submit."

Cam smiled. "The bond I have with Noelle is personal, so please forgive me if I don't discuss it. I will say this. I'd given up on finding anyone. I thought I would be alone, and I'd made peace with that. Noelle was a ray of sunshine in my life and for that I am eternally grateful."

Cam stepped back. "Tori, it is customary at a collaring ceremony for a submissive to be disciplined before the guests as an outward sign of her obedience and devotion. Do you wish to do this?"

Ian leaned down so only she could hear. "You don't have to do this, love. It's okay. Not all ceremonies end like this."

She looked up at Ian, her heart full of love. She nodded. "Yes, please."

Cam held out his hand and she placed hers in his. He helped her to her feet. "Congratulations to both of you. We'll step back and let you finish."

Ian took her hand and led her to the spanking bench. "You don't have to do this."

She gave him a mischievous look. "Don't I have several punishments coming to me? It's not like you to let me out of them."

He nodded, his expression turning stern, but his blue eyes were soft and tender. "True, slave. You do have several punishments coming to you." He pointed to the spanking bench. "I think you know what to do."

She did. She was practically wriggling with excitement as she climbed onto the bench and let him secure her wrists, legs, and ankles to the soft leather. He adjusted the bench until her ass was in the air. She was shocked he hadn't removed her thong, but grateful at the same time. She didn't want her pussy in her friend's faces. Some things shouldn't be shared with others.

She felt his hands rubbing her ass cheeks, warming up the skin. "Do you accept this punishment, slave?"

"Yes, Master. I accept this punishment."

He reached into his bag and pulled out a tube, opening it up and retrieving a riding crop. Her pussy clenched and honey started to drip from her cunt as she imagined how it would feel on her vulnerable bottom. She'd never had the crop before but had seen it used. It was going to leave some marks.

He held it in front of her. "Kiss the tool of your discipline, slave."

She pressed her lips to it and he disappeared from her sight, rubbing her ass again. He usually made her wait for it, but perhaps because of the observers he got right to it. The crop whistled in the air and then she felt a line of fire across her butt cheeks. She pulled at the restraints and whimpered at the unexpected sting of the crop. She'd been expecting more of a thud, like the floggers he had used.

"Where are we, Tori?"

She had to take a breath before answering. "Green, Master."

"Good girl. We'll continue."

Three more times the crop came down on her ass, and three more times she hissed at the burn. Her whole bottom was on fire, his stripes laid neatly in a row. She knew the next one was going to be on the crease of her ass, right where her thigh met the cheek. It was a sensitive spot and it was going to hurt like a bitch.

He leaned down and whispered in her ear. "Where are we? Do you need to use your safeword?"

"Green, Master."

"Close to yellow, love?"

She shook her head, realizing her voice had been shaky. "No, Master. We're green. I'm not looking forward to the next stroke. I know where it's going to land."

He brushed back her hair from her forehead. "We can stop now. You didn't need to do this in the first place."

"No, I want to do this."

He knelt there looking at her for a long time. Their guests had to be wondering what was going on.

"Why do you want to do this? Because you had a punishment coming? Because you want to show everyone your devotion and submission? You have shown them, not that's it any of their fucking business. And you're not going to be sitting comfortably this evening, so you've taken your punishment. So why do you want me to continue?"

Honesty was the cornerstone of any Dominant-submissive relationship. Lying to her Dom was a serious offense. She had to be honest. She'd come a long way since their first date.

"I want you to continue because as much as I hate it, I love it. I love submitting to you. I love the bondage. I love kneeling at your feet, feeling your love and protection. I even love this fucking crop which is turning my ass into a white hot flame. I love it. I'm aroused and I need you to keep whipping me. Please, Master?"

* * * *

Her admission set him on his heels. Her honesty was forthright, raw, and beautiful. She humbled him on a fucking daily basis. How did he get this lucky?

He stood up and nodded. "Then we'll continue."

Her bottom was a rosy red with four dark stripes running parallel. She was correct in her assumption of where the next stroke was going to land. He lined up the crop and brought it down right where the curve of her ass met her thigh. She half-screamed, and her hands and feet tensed in the restraints. He gave her no respite, laying the sixth and last stripe about an inch below the last. He rubbed the abused flesh and she whimpered as his fingers traced the stripes.

Her ass had to be on fire, but up close, he could smell her arousal. She was turned on. Time to get rid of their guests. He unbuckled her restraints, letting her catch her breath, and headed straight for Conor.

Conor understood immediately, rounding everyone up and practically pushing them out the door. Conor had arranged for them to have this room privately for as long as they needed it. If Ian had his way, they would be in it all night.

He helped Tori off the bench, looking her over closely to see if she needed a breather. Her hands started roaming over his chest and under his jacket. She was ready to keep playing.

He pulled her toward the St. Andrew's cross. "I have a special surprise for you. Let's get you set here."

He'd been planning it since they exchanged I love yous. He quickly popped the hooks on her corset and let it fall away before tugging her soaked thong down her legs. He lifted it to his nose and smiled.

"Someone liked her punishment. What do you think of the crop, love? It is a keeper?"

She wrinkled her nose. "I told you. I definitely have a love-hate relationship with that thing."

He laughed, clipping her wrists to the wooden *X*. "It sounds like the perfect implement for punishment then. I'll keep it handy." He bent down and spread her legs, clipping each ankle to the wooden planks. She was spread out and lovely. Her skin flushed and her eyes sparkled. She loved bondage most of all.

He reached into the leather bag and felt for the small ring box. He had another surprise for his beautiful woman. He stood in front of her and leaned forward, capturing her lips in a tender kiss. His heart ached with love. He dropped to one knee.

"You've accepted my collar, Tori. Will you accept my ring? I know when we started all this you weren't looking for a permanent commitment. Well, you've got one. From me anyway. Will you live with me for the rest of our lives and build a life with me? A partnership, Tori. A marriage of equals."

She pressed her swollen lips together, and her eyes were bright with unshed tears. "Equals, huh? Are you sure about that?"

He grinned. "Never more sure. Of course, there will be times when equal might mean something different than conventional wisdom says it is."

A smile broke from her lips. "Why doesn't that surprise me? Where might this be true?"

"In the bedroom, mostly. By the way, enjoy this while you can. This is the first and last time you'll see me kneeling at your feet, asking you to take pity on me. Damn, woman, are you going to put me out of my misery or not?"

She giggled and the sound made his heart do flips in his chest. He would make her laugh every day of their life.

"Yes, *partner*, I'll marry you. Now get off your knee. It just looks and seems wrong. Especially here."

He stood up and held the emerald-cut diamond up for her to see before reaching and placing it on her finger.

"Fits perfectly. Now on to my surprise. I think you're going to like this, little slave."

Ian opened a closet door and wheeled out the cart Conor had prepared ahead of time. It was filled with candles of different colors and sizes, plus a pitcher of water and a bucket of ice. He placed it so Tori could see, and her eyes went wide with delight. He lit each candle to let the wax start to pool and removed his jacket and tie, rolling up his shirt sleeves. He would need to test the wax on his forearm. The entire time, Tori's eyes were riveted to the candles, her nipples tightening and her tongue darting out to moisten her lips. He felt his groin tighten in response.

He needed to get control of his aching cock because it was going to be awhile before he got any release. Despite his dire warning at the beginning of the evening, his lovely slave was going to come long before he would. He wasn't going to tease her for long. Only enough to make her come for him. Hard.

"First, we need to warm you up a little bit."

* * * *

She was feeling pretty warm already. She could feel the heat from the candles, and her arousal had ratcheted up a million notches. Her pussy was flooded and her nipples were hard nubs in anticipation. She felt butterflies in her stomach, but they weren't from fear. Ian would keep her safe no matter what.

He nuzzled her neck and kissed and licked the skin on her neck and down to her shoulder before running his tongue to the sensitive skin under her arm. She giggled as he traced circles down her ribs.

"Ticklish, sweetheart?" He nipped at her hip bone. "You seem pretty warm. How about we get you hot?"

His warm lips traveled over her belly and down to her pussy, sending arrows of pleasure throughout her body and fire licking along her veins. She squirmed and bit her lip, trying not to beg. He had promised earlier she would be waiting for her pleasure tonight.

He kissed a trail up her inner thigh, swiping his tongue along her slit. She moaned as he made contact with her swollen clit, pulling at the restraints. She wanted desperately to touch him, run her hands all over his yummy body. He ran his tongue all over her dripping cunt, teasing her clit until she was panting and thrashing her head back and forth. He pulled his mouth away and stood, looking her up and down.

"I think you're ready."

He lifted up one of the white pillar candles, holding it high, and dripped some of the wax on his exposed forearm. He lowered his hand a few inches and dripped a little more before nodding.

"Do you want this, slave?"

The candle glowed in his hand and she licked her suddenly dry lips. "Yes, Master, I want it."

"Ask me for it."

She looked into his beautiful blue eyes, full of passion and hunger. "Please, Master. Please drip the wax down my body."

He moved close and lifted the candle above her shoulder, tipping it until the wax dripped down and splashed on her skin. The sear of the heat was immediate and then it was gone, a pleasant warmth left behind. She blinked in confusion. It had happened so fast.

He tipped the candle again and drew a long line from one shoulder to the other, the wax a thin line, hardening almost immediately. He stepped back.

"Where are we, slave?"

"Green. Very, very green, Master."

"What a pleasure you are to play with."

He smiled and tipped the candle again, splashing wax on her shoulder and watching as it dripped a few inches down her arm. He reached for another candle on the tray and quickly tipped the wax down the sensitive skin under her arm. She jumped as the heat lasted longer, then finally blew out her breath.

"Are we okay, slave?"

"Green. Please don't stop."

She forgot to use his title, but he didn't seem to notice. He began using different colors of wax to paint her shoulders, belly and thighs. She was a quivering, begging mess by the time he finished filling her belly button. He gave her a look of pure wickedness as he reached for an ice cube from the bucket.

"Time to cool you off. I don't want you to come yet."

He ran the ice all over her right nipple, and she sucked in a breath as the iciness contrasted with the warmth of the wax against her skin. He ran it all over the puckered skin until the nub was almost frozen. He tossed the cube away and lifted up a candle, the wax poised over the cold nub. Their eyes met and he tipped the candle, the wax landing squarely on the rosy flesh.

She closed her eyes and screamed at the sensation, the heat against the cold skin. Her cunt tightened in a small orgasm she couldn't control, and cream rained from her pussy. He picked up another ice cube and ran it around her other nipple, the anticipation making her whimper and moan. He picked up the candle again.

"You do not have permission to come. Don't think I didn't notice the baby one you snuck in a few moments ago. You know the rules, Tori."

She steeled herself, biting deeply into her bottom lip and clenching her fists to control her response. His expression was stern as he dripped the wax on her vulnerable nipple, the heat hotter than she'd expected against the icy backdrop. She cried out, desperately trying to control the pleasure racing through her. She was panting, her body pulling against the restraints. She'd never known arousal this intense was possible, never dreamed a human could stand this much pleasure.

He reached for another ice cube. "Where are we, slave? Do you need to safeword?"

She shook her head vehemently. "No, please, Master. I'm green. God, please don't stop."

He nodded. "You have permission to come, sweetheart. You don't need to hold back."

She sighed in relief then went up on her toes in shock when he applied the ice cube to her cunt, running it all over, through her folds and then over her sensitive clit. She was groaning and twisting as much as she was able to in the restraints, but she couldn't get away from the ice cube, cooling down her slit and raising goose bumps on her heated flesh.

He picked up a candle in each hand and tipped them until the wax dripped out of the well. It seemed to happen in slow motion. The wax dripped ever so slowly, her body pulled taut, waiting for the rush of heat. When it finally touched her clit, it was as if she had been licked by a tongue of flames. She screamed her release as Ian pressed an ice cube over the wax, immediately cooling it down and sending mixed signals of hot and cold, pleasure and pain to her brain.

The waves of pleasure shook her body and sent her someplace she'd never been. It seemed to go on forever, and then she was being carried over to the big bed. A bottle of water was pressed to her lips and she lay there limp and sated while he pulled off the wax off in big sheets. When he was done, he rubbed oil into her skin, removing the residue, before cuddling close to her. He pulled her practically on top of him and she sprawled on his large frame, letting her mind clear and her body stop shaking.

"Talk to me, sweetheart. Say something." Ian's warm breath was right next to her, tickling her skin. She reached up and ran her fingers through his golden hair, loving the freedom of movement and the silky way it felt between her fingers.

"I'm not sure I can even form words yet, let alone sentences. That was mind blowing. Wow."

He chuckled. "I'm glad you liked it. I told you tonight was a night you'd remember for a long time. We owe Conor a big thanks for the arrangements, and Cam for the ceremony."

She pretended to pout. "I thought I would remember it because of my punishments. Instead you give me a night worthy of a fairy tale."

He burst out laughing. "What kind of kinky, messed-up fairy tales are you reading, woman? There are chains and whips hanging from the walls and a closet full of sex toys. We didn't have stories like this when I was a kid."

"I guess it would be wrong on several levels, wouldn't it? Still, it's been a wonderful night." She sighed in contentment.

He pressed his hard cock into her hip. "The night isn't over, slave. Since you can talk now, I think I need to take your breath away. Again."

She ran her hand down his flat stomach and cupped his hard length through his pants. "Bring it on, Master mine."

He rolled off the bed and began to pluck at the buttons on his shirt, revealing the golden skin underneath. Her fingers itched to explore all the hard planes and muscles beneath the smooth flesh. He started to unzip his pants and frowned.

"You look a little too comfortable there, pretty slave. I think we'll have to do something about that."

Before she could catch her breath, he'd rolled her over on her belly and attached her wrists to her ankles. She was restrained, vulnerable, with her ass in the air for his taking. Her arousal spiked and her pussy dripped. She loved it.

She heard the crinkle of a condom and then felt the brush of his cock against her cunt. His hands were grasping her hips hard, his fingers biting into the soft flesh. He nudged the head of his dick at her opening, probing and teasing. She tried to push back, but he easily controlled her.

"Uh uh. I'm in charge, Tori. I decide when you get cock. Damn, is there anything sexier than you on your hands and knees waiting for me to fuck you? I don't think there is. Your ass is still a lovely red color from your punishment earlier." His fingers traced the stripes.

"Ask me for it, slave."

She was going to kill him later. She wasn't sure how, but her mind was whirring with visuals of pushing him off a cliff or at the very least kicking him between the legs. She was going to hurt him for teasing her like this.

"If you don't fuck me right now I'm going to poison your food," she said sweetly. "My handsome, sexy Master."

She had already started her climb to orgasm once again. Her body was primed and ready. She only needed his…input.

He threw back his head and laughed. "I'll say this for you, Tori. You don't have an ounce of self-preservation. I'll fuck you, slave, but you'll have another punishment coming, and your ass is still marked from the last one. I ought to come and leave you hanging tonight."

She scowled at him, not in the mood at all for his Dominant games. "That is so mean. We were engaged tonight."

"That's the only reason I won't leave you denied and frustrated, woman. Take heed. I earned the nickname the Devil Dom. I won't be so nice next time."

Before she could think of a retort, he thrust into her waiting pussy with one stroke. She cried out at the feeling of being so filled with his cock.

"Ahhh, oh God. It feels so good." She was already panting, wriggling her ass. He smacked the sore flesh and traced his handprint.

"You're so fucking tight and hot. I'm going to fuck you fast and hard, so hold on."

In the position she was in, she couldn't do much else. Her head was pressed to the mattress, her ass in the air, her cunt impaled with long, thick man meat. He pulled out and slammed back in, sliding over her G-spot and sending waves of pleasure straight to her clit. Their bodies were slapping together, her pussy clenching around his cock. She was poised on the edge, waiting to go over. His fingers played with her sensitive clit.

"Come hard for me."

She flew apart, her soul shattering into a million pieces. She screamed his name and she felt him stiffen, his cock swelling inside of her. They rode the wave together until he unfastened her restraints and pulled her close to his side. Their bodies were covered with sweat and her cream, and the room was filled with the musk of their sex. Candlelight flickered and cast shadows on their entwined limbs. Tori lay her head on his bicep and kissed his shoulder.

This was the man she loved. She hadn't planned it, but how lucky she felt to have found him. Right next door.

She ran her hand down his muscular arm. "I still can't believe we have our whole life to explore this passion, this connection between us."

He pulled her closer, his fingers combing through her long hair. "Believe it, sweetheart. I'm going to make it my mission in life to keep you happy. In and out of the bedroom."

She lifted up to gaze into his beloved face. "I'll do the same for you. After all, we're equals."

He gave her a slow smile. "Equals. Partners." He rolled her onto her back, his flesh hot against hers. "Except in the bedroom. Looks like we're in bed right now." His cock was already hard again and pressing into her belly.

She wound her arms around his neck. "Looks like you're in charge. You can do whatever you want to me."

She knew what he wanted would be what she wanted, too. They were two halves of a whole. She giggled and pressed herself closer to his hard body.

"Kiss me if you love me."

He pressed his lips to hers and the world drifted away to a place for just the two of them. Man. Woman. Master. Slave. Partners. Most of all, lovers.

THE END

WWW.LARAVALENTINE.NET

ABOUT THE AUTHOR

I've been a dreamer my entire life. So, it was only natural to start writing down some of those stories that I have been dreaming about.

Being the hopeless romantic that I am, I fall in love with all of my characters. They are perfectly imperfect with the hopes, dreams, desires, and flaws that we all have. I want them to overcome obstacles and fear to get to their happily ever after. We all should. Everyone deserves their very own sexy happily ever after.

I grew up in the cold but beautiful plains of Illinois. I now live in Central Florida with my handsome husband, who's a real, native Floridian, and my son whom I have dubbed "Louis the Sun King." They claim to be supportive of all the time I spend on my laptop, but they may simply be resigned to my need to write.

When I am not working, I enjoy relaxing with my family or curling up with a good book.

For all titles by Lara Valentine, please visit
www.bookstrand.com/lara-valentine

Siren Publishing, Inc.
www.SirenPublishing.com

CPSIA information can be obtained at www.ICGtesting.com
Printed in the USA
LVOW04s1659140615

442438LV00022B/791/P